Bliss
2

By

B.A. Talarico

&

Smurf

DEDICATION

I want to dedicate this book to my family, friends and everyone who has purchased the original Bliss. If it wasn't for you guys this wouldn't be possible. I want to make a special shout out to the people who made Bliss 2 possible:

Mackenzie Propst (main editor)

Kris Frigga (cover designer)

Marguerite Tomlin (assistant editor)

Claudette Melanson (print copy formatter & proofreader)

SMURF

"Come on Smurf, let's put the Remy in the kitchen," Tanya says, motioning for him to follow her. He sets the case of Remy on the counter and examines the condo. As he looks around the crowd of people, he notices a sexy Columbian girl approaching.

"Tanya!" the girl says, hugging Tanya.

"Hi Mindy," Tanya responds.

They release each other, and the girl's focus turns to him. "And who's this?"

"This is Smurf. Smurf, this is my little cousin, Mindy."

"Nice to meet you Smurf," Mindy says.

"Yeah, you too," he replies.

Mindy turns back to Tanya. "Hey, I need to run, Tanya. You know where everything is! I'll talk to you guys in a bit," Mindy says before taking off into the crowd.

They mix themselves some drinks and make their way around the condo and into a back room.

Inside they find a large glass table. Covering the table is a large 'C' in a white, powdery substance, a large 'E' in what looks to be multiple colors of ecstasy pills and a large 'W' in what has to be at least a half a pound of White-Rhino hypnotic marijuana.

He leans in toward her. "Are you serious?" he whispers.

She laughs. "Grab a nugget and roll a blunt. I'll be right back."

He nods and pulls a Swisher Sweet from his pocket. He grabs a fairly-large nugget off the table and starts breaking it down. Tanya returns with Mindy and a young, red-haired white boy.

"Can we smoke?" Mindy asks.

"Sure," he replies.

"Oh, before I forget, Smurf, this is my boyfriend, George. George, this is Tanya's friend, Smurf."

"Nice to meet you, Smurf," George says, extending his hand.

He accepts his hand. "Yeah, you too, Family." He returns his attention back to preparing the blunt.

They all sit, taking a couple puffs and passing it on. Mindy interrupts the silence. "So, Smurf, what do you think about the party?"

"It's alright... That stuff with the glass table was pretty funny. That be some shit you'd see in the movies," he replies, exhaling a huge cloud of smoke.

He passes the blunt and notices a young white kid in the corner of the room, talking to a group of people. He stares at him for a moment.

Man, I've seen him before...

Tanya notices Smurf's concentration and follows his gaze. "Smurf, are you good?" she asks.

"Yeah, I'm fine. That cat over there...looks familiar."

"The one up against the wall?" George asks.

"Yeah, him."

"Yo, JJ!" George yells. The kid turns and looks at George.

"You know that guy?" he asks.

"Yeah, I know him. That's my friend, JJ," George replies.

JJ leaves his corner and approaches their group. "What's up, George?"

"Hey, JJ, this guy thinks that he knows you."

JJ turns and looks at him. "Oh, really? From where?" JJ asks.

Smurf eyes him, thinking. "Have you ever been to Secrets, Family?"

"Yes, a few times," JJ replies.

"Did you ever spill a drink on someone?" he asks.

JJ's face turns pale. "Yeah...by accident."

"Well, that was me... I thought I recognized you."

"Yeah, I'm sorry."

"It's cool, Family. You want a hit?" he asks, passing the blunt to JJ.

"No, I'm good. I'm on paper… Only a few more months left, then the partying will start again. But I'm sorry, what was your name again?" JJ asks.

"Smurf," he replies.

"Okay, Smurf. I'm JJ. Nice to meet you."

"Yeah, you too, Family. Nice to meet you."

They finish the blunt and move into the kitchen. The Remy gets opened, and shots start flowing.

"Hey, Tanya, where's the bathroom?" he asks.

"It's down the hall on the left," she responds.

As he makes his way through the crowd of people toward the hallway, he runs into Mindy and a younger Colombian guy. "Hey, where are you going?" Mindy asks.

"Trying to find the bathroom."

"Oh, it's down there on the left. Across from the bedroom."

"Okay, thanks," he replies.

As he starts to walk off, she stops him. "What was your name again?" she asks.

"Smurf."

"Oh, that's right," she replies. "I'm sorry, this is my little brother, Quick. Quick, this is Tanya's friend, Smurf."

The two of them lock eyes. "What's up, Family?" Quick says.

He's stunned to have Quick, the man he's wanted to kill for Jeff's death, standing just inches in front of him. His rage keeps him from speaking. He just stares. He finally responds after getting himself under control. "What's up?"

Someone calls for Mindy from the living room. "I'm coming!" she yells back. "Ok guys, I gotta run. I'll talk to you in a minute." She turns around and disappears into the crowd again.

"What was your name again?" he asks. Quick tries to answer, but doesn't get much out before Smurf pushes him into the open bedroom. He follows him into the room and closes the door. He pulls out his gun and points it at Quick's head. "You have thirty seconds to explain what happened to Jeff."

"Hey, hey! Relax, dude! Just relax!" Quick pleads.

"twenty seconds," he says with no emotion.

"Okay, okay, okay! A couple of niggas used to buy from me...just a little bit at a time. Well, one day, they ask for some pretty heavy weight, and it was weight that I didn't have, so I talked to Jeff to see if he could hook me up."

"Keep going," he orders.

Quick continues. "Well, they wouldn't give me the money. They wanted to be there to see the stuff, so we were waiting for him to show, and a Tahoe shows up... I didn't know who it was, but before I could say anything, Leo and Teddy already had guns drawn and were unloading rounds into the SUV...so we all took off."

"Not good enough," he responds as he pulls the hammer on the gun back.

"Wait, wait! They said something about some guy named Junior being proud of them... They also said the name Smurf, too."

Smurf lets this sink in.

The hit was meant for me...

He stares down the barrel of the gun as the bedroom door swings open and smacks the gun out of his hand. Quick lunges for it, and they begin to wrestle.

"Hey, stop!" a female voice yells as the door closes. Both men look up to see a chrome pistol aimed at them. "What the fuck is going on in here?" Tanya yells as she switches facing the gun between Smurf and Quick.

Here's my chance.

While still on the ground, he reaches for his ankle holster and quickly pulls and aims the gun at Quick. "I want fucking answers!" he yells as he slowly gets up.

She turns and looks at him. "Let's put these things down, and we'll talk," she says, slowly lowering her gun.

"I ain't doing shit 'til dude puts the gun down first!" Quick responds.

"Smurf, put the fucking gun down!" she demands. He holds steady. "Put the gun down!" she yells. Smurf places the gun on the bed. "Now, what do you want to know?" she asks.

"You tell me," he replies.

"Okay...when you told me who Jeff went to meet, I took off to go talk to Quick to find out what happened."

"We pretty much established that already," he replies.

"Alright, well I needed to get close to Leo and Teddy, and he helped me...and you know the rest of it."

"So, it was you that killed Leo?" he asks. She says nothing. This only confirms his statement.

Damn, this girl is a bad bitch...and a smart one, too.

"So, is the shit squash now? Can we get back to the party?" she asks them.

"Yeah, Ma, we're good," he replies as he puts away his gun.

"Okay, good. Come on, let's get back to the party," she says as she opens the door. She waits for Quick to exit first, then follows. They return to the kitchen and continue taking shots of Remy.

Before long, they are back in the back room smoking more weed. Mindy breaks the silence again. "Let's pop some ecstasy, guys. I wanna party... Let's get crazy! Plus, George and JJ aren't always here, so let's have some fun!"

Tanya looks at Smurf. "Do you want to?"

He shrugs. "Fuck it, let's do it."

JJ gets up and heads over to what used to be an 'E' on the table. He scoops up some pills and returns. "Who wants to go first?" JJ asks, holding out his hand.

They start to grab the pills from him one by one. Smurf grabs his pill and looks at it. Just a chalky-white pill with a large number '1' stamped on it.

"Are these pretty good?" he asks.

"Yeah, they're pretty good," JJ assures.

He shrugs and throws the pill into his mouth.

Mindy looks at JJ. "Will you do a light show for us? I've heard you're really good!"

JJ laughs. "Sure." He bends down and undoes the laces from one of his shoes. He pulls out a pair of new glow sticks and ties each end of the shoestring to each glow stick. He bends the sticks and they crack. Bright, neon green shines through the plastic.

"Someone turn off the lights," JJ says as he moves an empty chair out of his way. Tanya gets up and turns off the lights, then returns to her spot next to Smurf on the couch. JJ starts swinging the glow sticks in a figure-eight motion in front of him. He continues this movement above his head and behind his back, flowing back to the front of his body. He starts bouncing the glow sticks off his arms. For JJ, it's just an activity, but for everyone rolling, it's a show of beauty.

"Wow, he's good," Tanya whispers into Smurf's ear. She rests her hand on his leg. JJ continues to swing the glow sticks, creating beautiful designs and trails. They sit in amazement, cheering and in awe over the spectacle.

JJ does this for fifteen minutes straight, then starts performing individual shows around the room.

When JJ gets in front of Smurf, he's stopped. "I'm good, Family," he says.

"Are you sure?" JJ asks.

"Yeah, looking good though."

"Come on Smurf," Tanya says.

"No, I'm good," he replies.

"Give me the glow sticks," she says to JJ. She takes the glow sticks out of JJ's hands and flips one of her legs over Smurf, straddling him. While sitting on his lap, she slowly starts to move the light to the beat of the song.

As she moves the light in front of his face, his eyes begin to follow the trails. It's as if he's in a trance. His eyes are uncontrollable as they follow the glowing light, but that's not it. He lets off a soft moan. Each time she moves, it sends sensations rushing through his body.

If this girl doesn't stop, I'm gonna end up fucking her.

The sensations keep filling his body. Tanya finally stops. "How was that?"

You have no idea.

"Great," he says.

"Good, I'm happy you liked it," she responds with a big smile. She pats his thigh with her hand.

A few hours pass, and he pops his last pill. The others do lines of ecstasy powder. "Are any of you guys thirsty?" Tanya asks. A few answer in confirmation. "Okay, I will get some water. Smurf, can you help me?"

He nods. "Sure, Ma, I got you."

They head to the kitchen and fill up a few glasses with water. "Here, take these to them for me, please," she says.

He grabs the glasses and takes them back to the room. Some time passes and he realizes Tanya never came back. He gets up and checks the kitchen, but no Tanya. She's not in the bathroom, either.

He starts checking other rooms and finds her in a bright red room with a large queen-sized bed, draped with a white comforter and four large fluffy white pillows lay atop of it. She's lying on the bed, listening to music. She looks up when he enters. "Hey, come in," she says, waving him in.

"And what are you doing in here?" he asks as he closes the door behind him. He walks over and sits down on the end of the bed.

She sits up. "How are you feeling?"

"I'm fucked up, but I feel great. How about you?"

"I feel great! Not a care in the world right now."

Satisfaction by Benny Bennasi comes across the speakers. "Oh shit, this is my song! Dance with me!" she says, jumping out of bed and pulling him to his feet. They begin dancing really close. The sensations are driving him to the edge. He moans as the song ends.

"You good at massages?" she asks. "I need one bad."

"Yeah, I am. Come on," he says, pulling her toward the bed. She lies down, and he starts massaging her neck, working his way down her back, then back to her neck. She flips her hair around her shoulder, leaving her neck bare. He slowly lowers himself, finding her neck with his lips.

He wakes up in bed with his arm around Tanya and notices he's only wearing his boxers. She's only in her bra and panties. He rubs his fingers across her soft, toned stomach. She stirs and pushes his hand down toward her laced panties. She lets off a soft moan.

Man, what the fuck happened last night?

He sees her move and lets his hands wander.

JJ

"Hey, George, did you get into contact with that lawyer?" JJ asks as they sit in his apartment, eating Subway.

"Actually, I did. I got a return call from him, and he said to call and set up a meeting to go in and see him."

"Okay, let's set up a time to see him. We need some legal backing for when we push out this new drug."

"Alright, I'll make the call and get it set up."

"You think that new drug could be smoke-able?" he asks George.

"I don't see why not. We would have to find a product to combine it with to make it smoke-able. It won't smoke in the current state it's in now... Why do you want to make it smoke-able, anyways?" George asks.

"Well, as I did my research for the molecular structure, I realized drugs can be taken in many forms...orally, anally, snorted, injected or smoked."

"And that means....?" George prods, looking confused.

"We need to make sure this drug can be used in all forms. If it can, this will be the ultimate drug...and *we* will own it! This will force every drug dealer to buy from us or one of our associates. We will eventually put all other types of drugs out of business, *and* it will be completely legal for us to sell!"

"JJ, you know you're nuts, right?" George replies as he starts to laugh.

"No, George, I'm being serious! Do you know how much the major cartels are making every year...pushing weed, powder, crack cocaine, ecstasy, heroin and meth?" He pauses for effect. "Billions upon billions... If we pushed them all out of the way with this, they would have to buy from us! Or kill us."

"Do you even hear yourself?" George asks. "You're talking about robbing multi-billionaire drug mafias! What's going to stop them from killing you?"

"I guess you're right," he responds.

"I mean... I don't hate you for dreaming, but we're just a couple of college kids. We're not cartel drug lords. We aren't important enough in the world to stay safe in a drug war that *we* will end up starting. I mean, look at all the major dealers...they either end up in prison for life or killed. I definitely don't want to be another number lost to the drug world. I want to be able to enjoy the riches from this stuff."

"Yeah, you're right, George. We have to crawl before we can walk.

Then we can run for the finish line."

"I mean, it's good to dream big, JJ...but if we can even get our stuff into major cities like Chicago, New York City, Miami and L.A., we're going to make millions upon millions! And I mean seriously, let's say we made $10 million each... We could invest in businesses or stocks and turn it into $20 million! We could live off the interest for life!"

"I never really looked at it like that, George... I just have big dreams for a life of riches and much more."

"I understand what you mean, but how are you going to enjoy the money if you're dead?" George says in a dark tone. JJ just looks at George sparingly with a blank look. George continues. "Because, JJ, your dreams are good too...but once you're dead, that's it. The game is over forever. Your life is priceless. No money in the world can bring you back from that."

"I know, I know," he replies as he looks down.

"We are partners in this, but I think we should just stick to keeping this in powder form and maybe figure out how to press it into pill form down the road. Let's leave the other stuff alone." George pauses to think. "I have a feeling it's going to end badly if we try to compete with the huge cartels."

"Yeah, George, you're right. Let's not get off track with this stuff. We still need to get more tests done." JJ stops abruptly, remembering something from earlier. "Actually, about that...there is a young hippie girl in my physics class that was telling me about an event in northern Iowa called Flower Patch."

"Flower Patch? What's that?"

"Well, from what she told me, it's a huge event. They have live bands, and people do drugs and party."

"Oh, like a drug festival?" George asked.

"Yeah! Exactly that!"

"When is this supposed to happen?"

JJ shrugs. "She told me in two weeks."

"Alright, so we need to get moving on getting this Bliss made... How much do you think we should make?"

"Not too much," he says. "Maybe 100...200 pills? We will sell them cheap...like $5 each...just to get people to try it."

"Sounds like a plan," George says smiling.

Over the next few days they begin producing Bliss. They reach their

200-pill goal amidst weighing and casing the powder in gel-caps.

George interrupts the steady production. "Hey JJ, I talked to that lawyer."

"What did he say?" he asks.

"Well, it's Tuesday... I told him we would come see him on Thursday to talk."

"Okay, that works for me."

"Alright... I wasn't for sure if it was good for you, but I set up the meeting anyway...just in case it was. So, now I don't have to call him again."

"Yeah. I'll plan to pick you up at your dorm. What time do we need to meet him?" he asks.

"I just went with 2:00PM on Thursday."

"Okay, I'll pick you up at 1:00PM, so we can get down there early."

"That's fine," George responds.

"Let's finish these pills. I'm beat," he says. They finish weighing and casing the powder, completely satisfied with their work.

Thursday comes sooner than expected. JJ and George pull into the parking lot of the lawyer's office and make their way inside.

JJ looks around the lobby at all the fancy, wood-trimmed items and plush couches.

Damn, this place is bad.

A pretty, blue-eyed woman with blonde hair is sitting at the front desk. "Hello and welcome to Goldman and Fitzer. How can I help you?"

George steps up to the desk. "Hi, we have a meeting with Dennis Goldman at 2:00."

She looks at the computer screen and answers, "Oh yes, there you are. Go ahead and have a seat. I will let him know you are here."

They nod and walk over to a light-brown, Italian-leather-couch. George looks at him. "What exactly are we going to ask him?" George whispers.

"I got a few questions prepared," he replies in a softer whisper.

The secretary walks over to their area and smiles. "Excuse me, you can go back now," she says while pointing towards a dark brown door. It looks antique, but fancy, and has a gold handle.

They get up, thank her and make their way to the office. An older gentleman is seated at a large desk. He looks to be in his mid-sixties, with salt and pepper hair that's cut short. He's dressed in a light-blue, long-sleeved shirt with red suspenders and tie.

"Come in, come in," the man says as he stands up to greet them.

"Hi, I'm George. We talked on the phone."

"Yes, hi. Nice to meet you, George."

JJ extends his hand. "Hi, I'm JJ. Nice to meet you."

The man shakes his hand and steps back. "I'm Dennis. It's nice to meet both of you. Go ahead and have a seat." They find seats across from Dennis. "So you guys wanted to look to me as, possibly, being a counsel for you?"

"Yes, Sir," George responds.

"You do both state and federal court, correct?" JJ asks.

"Yes, that is correct. I'm a criminal defense attorney in both state and federal courts."

"Have you ever represented drug dealers?"

"I've represented quite a few drug dealers...from illegal stops, to set ups by informants, to illegal searches that led to money confiscation by the authorities. What did you have in mind?" the older gentleman asks.

George sits quiet as JJ leans forward in his chair. "I did a little research on this, and I noticed it takes roughly a year to outlaw a new drug...is that correct?"

"In most cases, yes. But, if for any reason they feel a possible epidemic were to happen, they could outlaw it faster."

JJ leans back into his chair and whispers something into George's ear. George leans forward now. "What can we tell you and *not* tell you?" George asks.

"If you're doing something illegal, then don't tell me directly. Speak to me without incriminating yourself...like say 'someone who isn't me.' You know what I mean, Son?"

"Yes, Sir, I understand."

JJ leans forward again. "So, if, let's say...someone who isn't me, came up with a new drug that is at this point, still technically legal... Could they sell it legally?"

"Yes. Now, where they could mess up is not paying taxes, because the law could get them for tax evasion."

"So, legally, they could manufacture and sell this new drug?" he asks.

"Yes, as long as they are selling it as a new drug, and not a drug that is already illegal, and believe me, there is a grey area when it comes to that stuff."

"How much is your legal service to hire you as our counsel?" JJ asks as he sits back in his chair.

"Well, I would do $35,000 for a year...and that means if you have any legal questions or problems and need to do research, I do all of that for you. You can also contact me twenty-four hours a day, seven days a week. I will be on call."

"You pretty well connected?" JJ asks.

"Excuse me, Son?" Dennis replies.

"Are you well connected?" JJ asks again.

"Do you mean...Do I have authority to be able to find out if people are providing government agencies information in regards to you two?"

"Sure," he says.

The older gentleman leans forward in his chair. "Son, I've been doing this type of work for over thirty years. I have met and befriended many good people over the years. I think I can handle being your lawyer if you want me to be."

"Well, we need to discuss this. We'll contact you in the next day or two," JJ replies.

"Take your time. Just contact me when you come up with your

answer."

"Thank you for your time, Sir," George says.

"No, thank *you*. And call me Dennis."

"Yeah, thanks again, Dennis," JJ says.

"No problem, guys. Here's my card," he says, handing them each a card. "It has my e-mail, fax, work number and my twenty-four-hour-cell-phone number."

They thank him again and leave his office. They walk to the car without a word. George speaks as soon as they close the doors. "$35,000 is a lot of money, JJ."

"But it's worth it to keep one step in front of the law...and to have a lawyer at our beck and call twenty-four hours a day, seven days a week is something we need."

"Yeah, you're right. How much do you have saved, JJ?"

"I got more than enough to cover half."

"Okay, let's do it then. So that's $17,500 each?" George asks.

"Yeah, we'll do it that way. You cover half; I'll cover half."

"Alright, fine. I'll call him and let him know tomorrow, and you can run the payment to him, if that's cool."

"Yeah George, I'll drop off the money to him tomorrow."

"Excuse me, Sir, one of the gentlemen from yesterday is here to see you," the soft female voice says over the intercom.

Dennis pushes the talk button on the intercom. "Send him in."

JJ walks into the office, the money in his pocket. "Hi Dennis, sorry to disturb you."

"No worries. Come in and have a seat," Dennis responds.

"I just stopped by to drop off the amount we agreed on."

"Alright, good, very good."

"There's kind of a problem, though."

"What's that?" Dennis asks.

"Well, I have it for you...but it's all in cash."

"And we both know, if you mark $35,000 in cash, I'm going to have the IRS knocking on my door...so how do you want to do this?"

"Well, I'll give you the cash now, but you should show us paying the $35,000 over the next 12 months... It keeps people from snooping around. Will that work?"

Dennis takes a moment to think. "Well, JJ, I'm not really supposed to do that...but I'll do it this time."

"Okay, thanks Dennis. I really do appreciate it."

"No, thank you, JJ," Dennis replies. He watches JJ pull large wads of $100s from his pockets and place them on his desk. They both count the bills to ensure accuracy.

"So, we good?" he asks.

"Yes," Dennis says, piling the bills together. "It's been a pleasure doing business with you." He shakes JJ's hand.

"Before I leave, I need you to start researching chemical drug laws...how they decide if it is illegal or legal and so forth. Also, if you hear of them outlawing any new drugs, I want to be informed."

"Anything specific?"

"Yes, 2C-I, 2C-B, 2C-E, and AMT."

Dennis smiles. "I'll start looking into that for you, and I'll let you know what I find."

"Okay, sounds good. Thanks again, Dennis," he replies before leaving.

He pulls out his phone on the way to his car and sends a short message to George.

We are good.

"Where is this place at?" he asks George. They're in the car, surrounded by fields, a few buildings and winding gravel roads. One road leads to Flower Patch.

"She told me to turn right at a gas station with a white building next to it…and follow the road and will see it."

"Well, there's the gas station," he responds, pointing to a tiny building in front.

They turn right and follow the gravel road until they find a sign with the words, 'Flower Patch,' painted on it. They pull into the entrance and are immediately stopped by security. "Welcome to Flower Patch. I need to see some ID to verify you're both eighteen years of age or older, and it's $5 per person."

They give the security guard their IDs and a $10 bill. He looks over their IDs and hands them back. "Okay, thank you, guys. Enjoy your time," the security man says. They pull forward and find a place to park.

"Man, look at all the cars! There has to be like…500 people here!" he exclaims.

"Yeah, no kidding," George says.

"Hey, grab the stash-spot pop cans and let's go."

They walk up a walkway toward a large open field behind a bunch of trees. The field is filled with tents and people. JJ smiles and laughs. "This is like a drug dealer's dream!"

They melt into the crowd. There are so many people, many who are selling drugs, openly.

"LSD, $10 a hit!" someone yells from one of the tents.

"BC Bud, $80 a gram!" someone else yells.

"Ecstasy pills, $25 each!" another person yells.

George looks at JJ. "Are you serious? They just yell it out like that?"

"I guess that's how they sell it."

"Shit, I'm not doing that," George says with obvious discomfort.

"Don't get all sissy on me now. I'll do it," he says.

He turns back to the crowd of strangers. "I got Bliss, a research drug! $5 a hit! If you don't like it, I'll give you your money back!" he yells.

Some people just look at him; others continue walking. A young couple passing by walks up to them amidst the shouting. "What are you selling?"

"It's called Bliss, and it's $5 a hit."

"Did you say if we don't like it, you'll give us our money back?" the woman asks.

"Yes. I'm 100% sure you'll love it! But if you don't, I'll give you your money back. All I ask is that if you do like it, please spread the word!"

"Can we get two hits, please?" the man asks.

JJ pulls two hits out of the hollowed can and hands them to him. "Here you go. Enjoy!"

"Thanks! Are you guys going to be walking around or sitting somewhere?" the man asks.

"We'll be moving around. Just yell 'I'm looking for Bliss!' and we'll find you," he says smiling.

"Okay then! See ya!" they reply. They hand him $10 and walk away.

"Our first sale!" he says, laughing.

"Yet," George adds.

They continue to walk while JJ yells out his marketing slogan. They get a few curious customers interested, but there's so much going on. Then they hear it.

"I want Bliss!" someone yells.

George looks at JJ with wide eyes. "Do you hear that, JJ?"

"Yeah! Come on!"

They walk toward the voice calling out and find the first couple they sold to earlier in the night, sitting by a bonfire. "There you guys are!" the young man says. "It didn't work!" He can hardly contain his self with laughter. "Actually, it's still hitting us both pretty hard! This high is amazing! It feels as if you can turn it off and on when you want to!"

"That's because you can!" JJ replies.

"Really?"

"Yes! That's what makes this drug great! The ability to control it yourself."

"Well, this is one of the best drugs I've ever taken! You guys come here often?"

"Nope, first time."

"Oh...have you been selling a lot of those?"

"Not really...here and there."

"Well, can I get some more?"

"Sure, how many?"

"I'd like ten." JJ nods as George pulls out ten caps and hands them to the man. The guy pulls out a $50 bill and hands it to JJ. "Come on, sit down! You guys want a beer?" the man asks.

"Sure," they say in agreement.

Within minutes they hear another. "I want Bliss!"

"Bliss over here!" JJ yells in response.

A small group emerges through the crowd, and the one in front yells again. "Who has the Bliss?"

"Over here!" he yells again, waving his hand in the air.

The group makes their way to him. "You got it?" the front man asks.

"Yeah, I do. What's up?"

"Can we get some?"

"How many do you want?"

The man looks back at the group and back to JJ. "We want twenty."

JJ looks at George. George pulls out twenty pills and hands them to JJ. "That's going to be $100.

The man in the front pulls out five $20 bills. "Good," he says as he drops them into the man's hands.

"Thanks," the man says, and he follows his group back into the crowd.

Another hour passes, and a middle-aged man with dreads yells out, "Who has Bliss?"

"Over here!" he calls in response.

The man comes over. "You have that Bliss?"

"Yeah, what's up?"

"There are a lot of people trying to find you; I guess... You're the only one with it. How much are you selling it for?"

George and JJ look at each other with excitement. "$5 a hit," JJ says.

"How many do you have left?"

"Over one hundred or so."

"I'll give you $400 for one hundred of them."

"You got a baggy?" he asks the man.

"Yeah."

"Alright, deal."

The man places four $100 bills in his hand. JJ nods at George, who opens up the untouched pop can and dumps the gel-caps into the baggy. "There's one hundred and two here…two more for you," he says as he pulls out two more from the other, almost-empty pop can.

"Thanks!"

"What's your name?"

"I'm Vick."

"Well, I'm JJ, Vick."

"Cool, thanks again, JJ."

"Yeah, you too." He passes the money to George.

Damn, word travels fast.

He turns to George again. "What do you think, George? Not bad for one night."

"But still not as good as the other stuff," George says.

"Just wait, just wait," he says, taking a drink of his beer.

Soon, it will be.

QUICK

He's sitting in his newly purchased trap car, a black-on-black Acura RL with black-tinted windows. All he can think about are the recent events: Jeff's death, the tasks Tanya has him doing and the newly started war the family is in...

And I'm caught in the middle.

He takes a puff from the blunt in his hand.

"You okay, Family?" a young male in his passenger seat asks.

"Yeah, Fam, here you go," he responds as he passes the blunt to his partner.

The man takes a couple drags and exhales. "So, what up with that ecstasy? You got any more?"

"I will soon...hopefully in a few days."

"Okay, well let me know because these girls are in love with that shit," the man says, laughing.

A dark-colored car with big rims pulls up to the intersection across the street. Quick already knows who's driving.

Are you serious? This nigga...actually driving down here after all this bullshit.

His thoughts are interrupted by his partner. "Hey, Family, you okay? You look like you just saw a ghost."

"Yeah, I'm good. But hey, I got to take off. I'll get at you later, alright?"

The man takes one more puff and opens his door. "Okay, Quick, hit me up later." The car door shuts.

Quick watches the car pull away and begins to follow, trailing from a safe distance. He sees it pull into a driveway. A female exits the house and gets into the car. He sees Teddy's face and notices his arm in a brace of some sort.

What the hell happened to him? Was that from the night Tanya left with him...

The car pulls away again, and he follows it into a drive-in movie theater this time. He parks several cars away, still within perfect view. He watches the woman get out and head toward the concession stand.

Here's my chance.

He pulls a .40 caliber handgun from his glove box and loads a clip into the chamber. He secures it and gets out of his vehicle, walking casually towards the passenger side of Teddy's car. He opens the car door.

"Hey, Ma--," Teddy starts, stopping midsentence after seeing Quick.

Quick sees Teddy try to reach for his gun. He pulls his out first and clicks back the hammer. "Whoa, whoa! What you so jumpy about, Nigga? Not expecting to see me? And don't try reaching for your gun again, or you're going to find out why they call me Quick."

"What do you want, Quick?"

"You tell me, Nigga! You and your bitch-ass friend got me caught up in all this shit!"

"Fuck you, Quick! I know you set Leo up and tried to set me up with that slut cousin of yours!"

"Hey, Nigga, watch your mouth when you talk about my family!" he yells in anger.

"Fuck you and your family! I fucked the shit out of that bitch! I was about to kill her, but we were rudely interrupted." Anger slowly fills Quick's eyes and Teddy notices. "What are you going to do, shoot me? Your family is already dead where they stand. Smoke knows everything, so killing me isn't going to save you."

"Dead where I stand, huh?"

Teddy remains quiet for a moment, then continues. "It's just a matter of time before they kill all of you."

"Too bad you won't be able to see it in your lifetime," Quick replies as he pulls the trigger, pushing a round into the side of Teddy head. Teddy's body falls against the door, blood draining. "Now you know why they call me Quick. Oh yeah, and tell that bitch-ass nigga, Leo, I said hello."

He walks back to his car quicker, but stays casual. He gets back to his car and pulls away. That's when he hears a girl scream.

"Come on, hurry up! Get out of the way!" he yells inside the car. "Fucking traffic!" He passes a few cop cars heading towards the drive-in.

Fuck, that was close...where's Tanya at?

He picks up his phone and calls her. "Hello?" she answers.

"Tanya, where are you?"

"At home, why? Everything okay?"

"Yeah, I just wanted to talk to you. I'll come over."

"Okay, I will see you soon." He ends the call.

He sits down on the couch. "So, what's up?" she asks.

"Well...," he responds, pulling the gun out of his black hoodie. He sets it on the table.

"What did you do?"

He takes a deep breath. "Well, I was chilling in my new trap car, and guess who I saw?"

"Who?"

"That nigga, Teddy."

Anger creeps over Tanya's face. "You saw that nigga and didn't call?"

"Listen, Cousin, I followed him around and watched him pick up some bitch, and I saw he had on an arm brace."

She smiles at this. "Go on."

"Well, I caught up to him at the drive-in, and he told me we're all dead where we stand."

She laughs. "Oh yeah? How is that?"

"He said something about telling Smoke Jr. everything and that we were all dead."

"So what else happened?"

This time he smiles. "He learned why they call me Quick."

"You killed him? Was he dead before you left?"

"Yes. I watched him die."

"Good, is this the gun?"

He nods once. "Yeah."

"Okay, I will get you a new one, and I'll get rid of this one… We gotta do this right."

"Come on, cousin, I'm not stupid."

"Well, I got some extra clothes in the spare room. Get rid of what you got on and bleach your arms, just in case."

"I know, I know." He gets up to go change his clothes, and she pulls out her phone and sends a text to Smurf.

Where R U at?

I'm at home Y?

R U going 2 B there for a while? I want 2 stop by.

Yeah ma come on through. I'll be here.

OK see you soon.

"What's up?" he says as she walks in.

"I got something tell you. It's good…real good," she says without pause.

41

"Okay."

"So Teddy's bitch-ass is history."

Smurf looks a little surprised. "What? You catch him?"

"No, Quick did. He just told me, but he also said that Teddy told Smoke Jr. everything."

"Is this something to be worried about?"

"I'll take care of him myself... So, what's going on with you, Smurf?" she asks, changing the subject.

"Just chilling." Now he's the one to change the subject. "Hey, what's up with that ecstasy stuff? That was strong and clean... I've been hearing about a lot of demand for it recently on the streets."

"Well, Quick is the one selling it. You'd have to talk to him about it. I don't know much about that stuff."

"Okay, cool. I guess I will have to talk to him next time I see him at your place."

JJ

"Hey, Chris," he says as he walks into the apartment's office.

"Oh hi, JJ. How are you doing?"

"I'm good. You have a second?"

"Yeah, come in and sit down," Chris says, waving him inside. "What's going on?"

"Well, first, here is that cash I owe you," he says, pulling a stack from his pocket. He hands it to him.

"Thanks, JJ, I appreciate you helping me out."

"Yeah, no problem. Thank you for helping me out as well."

"So, what did you need to talk about?"

"Well, I wanted to ask you...you're going to school for CPA, right?"

"Yeah, that's my major. Why?"

JJ avoids the question. "Are you pretty good at it?"

"Well, I'm not a 4.0 student by any means, but I know my stuff. Why? Are you looking for an accountant?"

"Yeah, I need help with something... How much they pay you here? $15,000 a year?" He doesn't wait for an answer. "Well if you help me, I will give you double...plus allow you to do this job... So you would get

$45,000 a year."

Chris looks wary. "You're going to pay me $30,000 a year to be a CPA for you?"

"Yes."

"What do I need to do?" Chris asks.

"Well, I have a lot of cash coming in, and I need to open some businesses that deal in cash so I can get it taxed."

Chris stares at him for a moment. "You know what you just asked me is considered money laundering, right?"

"It is?" he asks. He knows this of course.

"Yes...where is this money coming from? If you don't mind me asking."

He looks at Chris. "You don't need to worry about that. So are you in or what?"

Chris leans back in his chair and thinks. He leans forward again, this time, smiling. "I'm in."

"Good, good," he says, shaking Chris's hand. "I need a few businesses to move this money."

"Well, let me put it to you in layman's terms, JJ... There are a million and one ways to launder money. How much are you trying to do?"

"$100,000 and up."

Chris pauses. "Well, we can open a party company... We'll lie and say a ton of people show up and then wash the money. That way we can get a connection at the clubs."

"I got that, no worries," JJ reassures.

"Okay, well if we have enough, we can open a construction company and launder it through labor costs and so forth."

"Do we need a lot to legally open these businesses?"

"We can open with little to none, actually," Chris says. "We can take out loans and just pay it using the money we have."

"Really?"

"Yeah, and if you get really big, you can build some nonprofit businesses, like development centers and job-training programs...and you can get government grants to do it. Plus, that help gets you into the political world, because you're helping create jobs."

JJ's impressed. "Where did you learn all this?"

Chris shrugs. "Research...and from textbooks."

"When can you start doing the work for me?"

"I can start anytime."

"Okay, I need to see something real fast. I'll call you in an hour."

They exchange numbers, and JJ leaves the office.

He goes back to their lab in the rented apartment to find George hanging out. "Hey, George, we need to talk."

"What's up?" George asks.

"Well, I'm wanting to start opening businesses so we can wash this money."

George looks confused. "What? How are we going to do all that?"

"I'll take care of it. You're in though, right?"

George nods. "Yes."

"Okay, just, whenever I need your info, I'll let you know."

George gives him a weird look and shrugs. "Okay."

JJ pulls out his phone and calls Chris. "Hello, this is Chris."

"Hey, Bro, it's JJ."

"Oh, hey!"

"What do you need from us to open that party business?" JJ asks.

Chris and JJ exchange information. He can hear Chris writing over the phone. It's long and tedious, but it needs to be done.

Then, the final question. "What do you want the name to be?"

JJ had thought about it earlier before calling him. "L.K.E."

"What does it stand for?" Chris asks.

"Lady Kappa Entertainment."

JJ hears him writing again. "Okay, well, it's all set up," Chris confirms. "You guys are fully legal now. All you have to do is throw a party!" Chris says.

"Okay, thanks, Chris."

"Yep, not a problem. Hit me up when you need me!"

Everything is falling into place. Their small drug family is starting to show a profit after throwing a few really crazy parties at Club E. They feature DJs like Your Boy Dru Soy, Pri Yon Joni, DJ Bigboii, and the sexy female DJ Glaze. L.K.E is making $3-$4000, and laundering $10-$15,000, off each event.

The ecstasy keeps getting pumped through the parties, and the money keeps rolling in, but they soon realize they can't keep up. They open up another business doing new home construction for Section 8 and low-income families. With the party business and the construction company, JJ and George are raking in over $100,000 every few months in drug funds. On top of that, they are bringing in $30,000 a month in profit from the businesses. They aren't even twenty-five years old yet.

"This is Chris," Chris answers.

"Hey, Chris, it's JJ."

"Hi, buddy, what's up?"

"I want to start buying things."

"Okay, what do you want to know?"

He pauses. "Well, I can't draw attention...so how much can I spend and still stay under the radar?"

"Well, with how the books look, you and George can spend $10,000 each...but I would only spend half and invest the other half in a Roth IRA."

"Roth IRA?" This is new to JJ.

"It's an investment...kind of like a 401K."

"Oh," he says, feeling a bit silly.

Chris continues. "That is what I would do if I was you guys."

"Okay."

"So, $5,000 then...is that what you want to do?"

"Yeah, thanks for looking out for us."

"Well, that's what you pay me for, buddy! Have a good one!"

Within a couple months, JJ is reaping the benefits of his businesses. He buys a two-story, 4,000 square foot house, just outside of town, for him and Stacy, along with matching his-and-hers Mercedes SL 500 Roadsters. The next big purchase comes in the form of another house, which is used solely for the manufacture and distribution of powdered ecstasy and Bliss. The sky's the limit, and L.K.E isn't slowing down anytime soon either.

"Hey, George, you think the Bliss is ready?" he asks as they lounge on his back porch.

"I, personally, think we just need to make it, and when people want the ecstasy, we give them both.

We need to get people to start using it enough to cover what we are making off ecstasy."

He nods. "Okay, let's start sending an ounce of Bliss with every order to our dealers for them to try." George nods in agreement. JJ looks out over the backyard. "George…did you ever think we would make it this far?"

"Honestly, JJ, not really... This is a whole life change for us. We just have to remember what we said in the beginning: Make our money and get out."

He slowly nods his head in response. The power of greed is slowly taking him over.

"Bro, you okay?" George asks.

JJ is brought back to reality. "What? Yeah, just thinking of something."

"What about?"

"We've been hard at this for a while... I think we need a break. A little vacation would be nice."

"Where to?" George asks.

JJ thinks for a minute. "I was thinking either Miami or Las Vegas."

"Well, Miami sounds good! Mindy's family is from there. We can visit them!"

JJ nods. "That sounds cool. Call Mindy to see when she'll want to go," he tells George. He turns towards the door and calls for Stacy.

Yeah?" she yells. George walks off to call Mindy when Stacy steps onto the deck. "You needed me?" she asks.

JJ smiles up at her. "Yeah, you want to go on a vacation?"

"Where to?"

"Miami."

Stacy's eyes light up. "Oh my gosh! Yes, yes, yes!" she says, jumping up and down. "With who?" she asks.

"George and Mindy."

"Yeah! That will be fun! I've never been to Florida before!" she says in a super-excited voice.

George returns and sits down. "So what did she say?" he asks.

"She said it sounded like fun... She's free whenever."

"Well, it's Tuesday today," JJ says. "Let's plan to go Friday. We'll rent a private jet, go get her in Chicago and head to Miami."

"You sure we can afford that, JJ?" Stacy asks.

"Don't worry about it," he replies.

Then, it's settled!" George says. "We'll go Friday!" George looks down at his phone as it vibrates. He takes a few seconds to read his screen. "Mindy wants to know if Quick and Tanya and her friend can come, too?"

"Yeah, but they need to pay some money, George," he replies.

George goes back to his phone and, within a few minutes, he gets another text from Mindy. He reads it. "They said they will take care of food and drinks in Miami."

JJ nods. "Okay, that's fine." He sits back. A vacation is just what they need.

They meet their rental jet at the Ames airport and fly off to Chicago. Tanya, Quick, Smurf and Mindy are there waiting.

"This is nice!" Tanya says as they board the jet.

"Yeah, Family, this is dope. How much it cost?" Smurf asks.

"Not too much... George and I just got a good rental rate on it," JJ says.

The plane takes off with swift force and within hours they are at the Miami International Airport. Tanya's mom is there to receive the group, and they all pile in her new Cadillac Escalade EXT. Tanya hops in the passenger seat by her mom and gives her a hug.

"Everyone, this is my mother, Mia. Mom, this is everyone."

"Hi, guys," her mom says in a soft, soothing voice.

"Hi, Auntie," Mindy says.

"Hi, Honey, your parents are at home. We're going there first thing.

You guys can go check into the hotel afterwards."

They pull up to a large, gated house in the Coral Gables area. Mia drives up the wraparound driveway to the front door and everyone hops out.

"This is your parents' house?" George asks Mindy.

"Yeah," she says smiling.

"What do they do for a living?" JJ asks.

"We own an import-export business...one of the largest in Miami."

Smurf gives Mindy a crazy glance, looks at the house again, and then at Tanya. When they enter the house, he turns to George. "Damn George! Your in-laws got a house that could be on MTV Cribs!" George stays silent as he admires the house.

I thought I was doing a big thing... This is a whole other level.

Smurf leans into Tanya to whisper. "Damn, your cousins are rich! This is one of the biggest houses I've ever been in!"

"Yeah, it's pretty nice," Tanya replies.

Everyone chats among themselves upon entering the house. JJ breaks from the group and asks Mindy's mother for a phone book. Quick is first to jump in. "Yeah, I'll go get it," Quick says, getting up.

He brings back a large phone book and hands it to JJ. "What are you looking up?" Quick asks.

"Exotic car rental companies. I want to rent an exotic sports car for the weekend."

Quick looks surprised. "What type of car do you want?"

"A Ferrari F430 convertible."

"Well, I got a friend whose parents own a company like that... Let me call him and see what I can do for you."

JJ closes the book. "Okay, thanks, Quick."

"No problem."

Food is prepared and they eat until full. Quick looks down at his phone, then at JJ. "Hey JJ," Quick says.

JJ looks up. "You talk to your friend?"

"Yeah, he said he has a dark-silver F430 with red interior."

"How much for the weekend?" he asks.

"Well, they do it for $2,000...but if you give him $1,000, he'll take it."

"Okay, let's do it."

Quick nods once. "Alright, let's go."

JJ turns to George. "Hey, George, come with us."

"Where are we going?" George asks.

"Come on, just come with us," JJ replies.

Quick turns to Smurf. "You too, Smurf," Quick says.

Smurf shrugs and stands up. They all climb into Mia's Porsche SUV.

"Where are we going?" George asks again.

"It's a surprise," JJ replies.

They pull into the lot at Empire Corsa Club of Miami. A young Colombian kid in his mid-twenties, with black hair, waves to them. He's skinny and dressed in a T-shirt and jeans. "My boy, Alex! How are you are you liking Chicago?"

"I love it, David. You'll have to come someday when the weather is nice. These are my friends. This is JJ, Smurf, and Mindy's boyfriend, George."

"Oh, you're dating Mindy? You lucky dog! She's a great girl," the kid says.

"Thank you," George replies.

"So, who wanted the F430?" David asks.

"I did," JJ responds. "How much do I owe you?"

"$1,000," David responds. JJ pulls out $1,000 in hundred-dollar bills. David pulls out the keys and tosses them to JJ. "Go ahead and start it up," David says.

He opens the door and sits inside the car. The smell of the Italian leather fills his nostrils. He starts the car, and the howl of the purring engine sends chills up and down his spine.

Smurf looks on, impressed. "Damn, family! After hearing that, I gotta get me one, too." Smurf looks around the lot. "I see you have a charcoal-gray Aston Martin Vantage convertible over there... Is it available for rent?" Smurf asks.

"Yes, it's available," David says.

"I'll take it," Smurf replies, pulling out a large wad of cash.

JJ nudges George. "Come on, George, live a little!"

Smurf chimes in with JJ. "Yeah, Family, live a little! You're in Miami! Be whoever you want to be!"

George scans the area. "Well, I like that one," George says, pointing at the midnight-blue Lamborghini Gallardo Spyder.

"Well, you're getting it," JJ says as he pays David another $1,000 in cash.

They fill out the paperwork, and David gives them a crash course in how to use the paddle shifters. They're like children in a toy store.

"One more thing, guys," David says before they leave. "All I ask is please don't wreck them and don't beat on them too badly."

JJ smiles. "Trust me, we won't. Thanks again, David."

They follow Quick down Collins Street where pedestrians watch them in amazement. At a stop light, George opens his phone and reads what JJ sent him.

I can definitely get used to this!

Me 2 JJ. Me 2!

He presses SEND.

SMURF

They awake after a long night of partying and make their way down to the hotel lobby.

"What y'all wanna do today?" Smurf asks.

"Can we go to the beach?" Stacy asks.

"Yeah, let's do that!" George says, giddy. "I've never been to a beach before!"

"That's it then," Mindy says. "Let's all get ready and meet back here in a half hour."

The half hour passes, and everyone trickles into the lobby. Tanya turns to Mindy. "Call Quick."

"Is he going to meet us now?"

Tanya shrugs. "I called earlier."

Mindy goes to her phone and makes the call. She waits a few seconds before speaking and then turns away from Tanya. A few more seconds pass, and she ends the call and turns to face her again.

"He's still sleeping... I woke him up. He said to just go ahead, and he'd meet up with us for lunch later."

"Okay," Tanya replies.

"Let's go," JJ says as he heads for the sliding glass door at the entrance of the hotel.

They all make their way into their rented cars and drive towards South Beach. Tanya's riding with Smurf. He looks at her and then back to the road. "Tanya?"

"Yeah?" she responds.

"Do you know anything about Mindy's boyfriend…or his buddy?"

"I don't know much. I just know they both go to ISU in Iowa for chemical engineering."

He chuckles. "Oh, so they're nerds?"

Tanya laughs. "Uh, yeah. That's what Mindy says. Why?"

He shakes his head quick. "Just curious."

They get to the beach and spend the next few hours lying out and playing tag in the water. The day wanes, but the night hasn't even started.

"What do you guys want to do tonight? The club?" JJ asks.

"Which one you got in mind?" Smurf asks.

"I was thinking about, maybe, going to the Mansion. I heard that place is hopping down here!"

"Well, it is one of our last nights in Miami," Smurf replies. "We might as well go out in style."

Mindy's phone vibrates from an incoming text. She reads it and relays the message. "Hey, guys, Quick said to meet him at home."

Within minutes they are at Mindy and Quick's. They sit outside by the pool, which overlooks the ocean. There are yachts and speedboats by every home.

Smurf admires the marine vessels.

Damn! There is a lot of money to be made down here...

His thoughts are interrupted as Quick and his father join them. "Hey, guys," Quick says. His father begins to say something in Spanish to Tanya.

Tanya nods. "Sí, uno momento," she responds back to her uncle.

She speaks Spanish?

"I didn't know you spoke Spanish," he finally gets out.

She laughs. "You never asked! But I'll be back." She gets up and follows her uncle back into the house.

"So, what's up, guys?" Quick asks.

"Shit, nothing," JJ responds. "We're planning to hit up the Mansion tonight... You're coming with, right?"

"Fuck, yeah! My boy is the bouncer there, so no waiting in line!" he says, smiling.

"And bottles on me!" Smurf adds.

"Yeah! We're doing it big tonight!" JJ says with excitement.

"Yeah, what he said!" Smurf says, laughing.

"Smurf, I'll match you on bottles tonight."

"No, Family, I got this... You paid for the plane. I got this." Tanya returns and sits beside him. "Is everything good?" he asks.

"Yeah, they just needed help with something," she responds.

He looks at her with skepticism. He doesn't believe her for a minute. He can tell something is wrong.

I know her better than she thinks.

He turns to JJ. "So, Family, what is it you do? If you don't mind me asking."

JJ shakes his head. "It's cool. I'm in college, but I do some freelance pharmaceutical work on the side. What about you? What do you do?"

Smurf smiles. "I'm in the wholesale business."

JJ smiles, but stops when his phone vibrates. "I'll be back; I need to take this."

"How you liking Miami, Smurf?" Quick asks.

"Great, I almost want to move down here," he says.

Quick gives a small nod. "Yeah, it's nice down here, that's for sure."

"Hey, Quick, since I got you alone, I wanted to ask you... What's up with that ecstasy you get? I been hearing a lot of need for that back in Chicago."

Quick looks around nonchalantly. "I get some, but not a whole lot... Most of my stuff is presold. I can't keep it on hand. It moves too fast. Why?"

"Well, I want in. I got the money to keep it flowing, but I don't mess with that too much."

"Don't worry about it. We'll talk more when we get back home."

"Well, JJ is the person you need to talk to."

Smurf looks surprised. "The JJ that just went inside?"

Quick nods. "Yes, but chop it up with him later. This is just a vacation--no business, just relaxation."

The club is packed when they arrive later that night.

Quick said no waiting in line...thank God! The line is almost a block long...

He follows Tanya through the giant metal doors. "Fuck, this spot is huge!" he says in awe.

They head to the V.I.P section and crack open a couple bottles of vodka. After hours of drinking, dancing, and smoking, it's last call. They continue the party back at the hotel. Quick leaves with a girl he met that night, and soon after, everyone else starts to trickle back to their rooms.

Smurf and Tanya go to their room, but Tanya isn't ready for the night to end. She changes into a pair of booty shorts and a tank top and starts dancing around the room. Smurf watches her and smiles. She pushes him down onto the bed and starts giving him a lap dance, slowly gyrating her hips around his crotch.

Damn, this girl is sexy as fuck!

She turns and straddles him and begins rubbing her hands all over his broad shoulders. He leans in and kisses her softly on her moist lips. Their kisses become more passionate and hungry. She pulls his shirt off and throws it onto the ground. He picks her up and tosses her on the bed, a soft moan escaping her lips. He starts kissing her neck softly, making his way lower. He pulls her breasts out of her tank top, licking each nipple ever so slowly.

He continues south with his tongue and stops right above her pussy. He tugs her panties off and tosses them to the floor, planting kisses down her legs to her feet. As he makes his way back up, he spreads her legs until he fits perfectly between them.

Damn...Ima tear this shit up!

He begins licking her pussy. He spreads her lips and feels the hot wetness. She lets off a loud moan, and he continues to lick her swollen clitoris. He slowly slips two fingers deep into her, and she moans again, arching her back. He finds her G spot and rubs in slow circles.

"Fuck, keep going...faster," she moans. He obeys. The shaking in her body shows him she's nearing orgasm. "Oh, shit...I'm going to come!" she yells. Within seconds, she's squirting her female orgasm all over him. She pulls him down onto the bed. "Now it's your turn," she whispers.

She undoes his pants and pulls them to the ground. She rubs her breasts all over his penis and starts to lick the shaft. Fully erect, he is ready to go. He pulls her up toward him, and she helps the head inside her.

"Go slow, first," she moans. She closes her eyes and takes him in. He feels himself go deeper and deeper inside her until he is completely in.

"Fuck, Ma," he moans as he starts to thrust.

"Right there, Smurf... Oh, fuck!" she moans.

"Let me hit that doggy-style," he says.

She moans again and lets him pull out. He turns her around and slips inside again. His thrusts are already fast paced. He pulls her by her hair and smacks her ass.

"Yeah...like that," she moans. "Faster..." He starts pumping her faster and harder.

"More," she moans.

He lets off a deep moan, on the brink of climax.

"Yeah, Smurf...fuck me, Daddy! Come all over me, Daddy," she moans.

Fuck, I think I love this girl.

He continues pumping and is surprised when she reaches back. She starts massaging his balls.

"Oh fuck..." he moans. The sensations move from his toes, up through his legs.

"Yeah, Daddy, come for me..."

"I can feel it... Shit, I can't hold back any longer!" he moans. He pulls out and explodes all over her sexy back.

"Let me see that," she moans. She takes his dick in her hands and sucks it dry, swallowing.

"Now, how was that?" she says with a smile. She gets up and heads towards the bathroom.

"Fuck, Ma...words can't describe how great that was," he says between short breaths.

Tanya's mom arrives to pick up the girls at the hotel. The guys still have to drop their cars back off before returning to the airport.

"Before we drop off the cars, let's do a lap or two down Ocean Dr. and Collins...just for the hell of it," JJ suggests.

"Yeah, one last time to end a perfect weekend!" George responds.

Girls stare as they cruise Ocean Drive. It makes Smurf love Miami even more.

Half-naked girls running around, awesome beaches... What's not to love?

Pedestrians look on as they stop at a red light. JJ revs his Ferrari, which excites a crowd of people. They begin cheering loudly to the loud howl of George's Lamborghini. Smurf waits, smiling. A pair of designer shades cover his eyes. He revs up his Aston Martin, and more cheers erupt from the crowd.

They follow Quick to Empire Corsa Club of Miami where they drop off the cars and thank David for the hook-up. They climb into the Porsche SUV and speed off towards the airport.

"Man, Bliss would be a hit down here!" George says to JJ. JJ elbows him in the chest, signaling for silence.

Smurf overhears the comment from the back seat.

Bliss...what's Bliss?

"What was that for, JJ?" George asks.

"Shh...we will talk later," JJ whispers to George.

The girls are there waiting when they arrive at the airport. Everyone says their goodbyes, and they board the plane.

The flight feels like it takes a lifetime.

It's been a few days, but Smurf can still feel the sand in his toes. He's at Mindy's, rolling a blunt, when Quick walks in.

"Hey, Family, what's good?"

Quick takes a seat on the couch by him. "Nothing, what's up?"

"Shit," he laughs. "You know how we talked about that ecstasy stuff?"

"Yeah," Quick says, taking a baggie out of his jacket and adding some weed to Smurf's pile.

"Did you talk to JJ about it?"

"Not really."

Smurf keeps working on the blunt, but continues. "I figured that you could get ahold of him and get like...1,000 pills, and I'll pay for it...and you stick with just selling it."

"I'll get it in powder form, so it would be like...four ounces for 1,000 pills."

"That's fine. Get what you need, and we'll just do it like this for now. I'm busy with the cocaine game, so you take care of the ecstasy. Cool?"

"That works for me," Quick says. "I usually can't keep that stuff on hand...it goes so fast."

He smiles. "Good. That means easy money for the both of us!"

Ecstasy is a big hit in Chicago over the next few months. The city is flooded with pills that people are literally fighting for. They dish it out, and Mindy stashes the money. The system has proven useful so far, and Smurf considers Quick a reliable partner.

On a routine drop off, he stops to ask Quick a favor. "Hey, Quick, I'd like to talk to JJ in person... Could you set it up?"

Quick looks at him confused. "Is something wrong?"

"No, I've got a few things I would like to discuss with him in person...if possible."

Quick considers for a moment. "I'll call him and see when he can meet."

"Just let me know," he replies as he heads for the door.

Only an hour passes before he gets a text from Quick saying JJ will be in town this weekend.

Okay good to hear. Talk to you soon.

Smurf presses SEND and closes his phone.

JJ.

"Who was that?" George asks, not taking his concentration away from his video game.

"That was Quick... I guess him and Smurf want to meet with me this weekend," he says.

George frowns at the screen. "For what?"

He shrugs and heads down the hallway. "They didn't say. So, I'll go see my folks while I'm there and meet them to see what they want."

"Do you want me to come with?" George asks.

JJ rummages through cupboards, grabbing supplies for his trip. "No," he calls out from the bathroom. "Just keep pushing out the powder while I'm gone." He pops his head out of the bathroom to look at George. "Oh...and keep your mouth shut about the Bliss stuff... When we were in Miami, you were talking too much."

George's attention to the screen quickly switches to JJ. "Well I--" George starts.

JJ puts a hand up to stop him. "No, it's cool, George. Just from here on out, keep it on the down low... Loose lips sink ships. Shit like that will get us busted. That is all those people need from us... One slip and we're done."

George nods slowly. "Okay...I will stop talking about it."

The weekend comes faster than expected. JJ arrives in Chicago where Quick is waiting to pick him up.

"How was the flight, JJ?" Quick asks.

"It was good... Where's Smurf?"

"He's at home. We'll head over there now."

JJ watches the city fly by, reminiscing about his younger years. Before long, they pull up to a single-story house on a quiet street. JJ follows Quick up to the door, and they enter without knocking.

Smurf is sitting on the couch. "Come on in; have a seat." He looks to JJ. "Thanks for coming so soon, JJ."

"No big deal," he says, finding a seat across from Smurf. Quick sits next to Smurf and pulls out a baggie and some wraps. "I figured I would come see my folks anyway, too... So what's up?"

"Straight to the point... I like that," Smurf says, smiling. His demeanor turns serious as he continues. "We've been doing a good business with that ecstasy... We can't seem to get enough."

"So, you need more?" he asks. "I can get you more at any time. How much were you trying to get?"

"Probably 10 to 15,000 pills' worth," Smurf replies.

"I can do ten ounces for like... $1.50 a hit, which would be somewhere in the ballpark of...about $17,000 for the ten ounces. Is that cool?"

Smurf thinks about it for a second. "Yeah, that's cool. You still gonna ship it, right?"

"Yeah, don't worry about that, Smurf. I'll take care of that."

"Okay, good, we'll take it," Smurf replies.

"Okay, I will get it set up when I get back."

Quick is putting the finishing touches on a joint. "Hey, JJ, follow me real quick... I want to talk to you alone," Smurf says, quietly, as he gets up.

JJ nods and follows Smurf out to the back patio. "What's up?" he asks as Smurf closes the sliding glass door behind them.

"Well, I overheard your friend George saying something about some shit called Bliss when we were down in Miami."

Fucking George and his loud mouth.

"Oh, Bliss…yeah," JJ says, trying to sound a little confused.

Smurf just looks at him. "I know that you know what I'm talking about. I can see it in your face, JJ. There's one thing I'm about."

"And what's that, Smurf?"

"Getting money. And I just want to let you know that if you got something that makes money, I want it. I can sell anything… That's what I'm good at. Hell, I can probably sell a condom to a nun if I had to!"

He laughs. "A condom to a nun, huh?"

"Anything," Smurf replies. His confidence is radiant.

"Okay, I'll tell you what… When I send you this next batch of powder, I'll send you one ounce of Bliss for free. You can give it out and try to wrangle more buyers… If that goes good, then we'll talk. "But…do NOT give it out for anything other than *oral use only*…and no more than one hundred milligrams per hit. This is considered a research chemical, so, very few people have this. I just happen to know someone who does."

Smurf smiles. "Good, we'll discuss it more. Cool?"

"Yeah, that's fine."

They give a quick handshake and head back to the living room. They take up their original spots, and Quick passes the joint around.

After a couple puffs, he turns to Smurf. "You own a business or anything?" he asks, passing the joint to him.

Smurf accepts, but shakes his head. "Nah, Family. I'm not into all that shit. Why do you ask?"

"Well, if you're making a lot of money, I got a guy who can help you launder it... It will cost you, but you'll be able to do whatever you want and not have to worry about the feds coming to your house."

Smurf looks intrigued. "How much?"

"$30,000."

"Did he do it for you?"

"He has helped me open a few businesses, so, yes."

Smurf pauses. "Alright, Family. I'll think about it."

JJ takes the joint from Quick and inhales before speaking. "Well, if you do, I'll get stuff set up, and you can come meet him."

"Alright. So how long are you in town for?" Smurf asks, accepting the joint from JJ again.

"Just the weekend, then I'll be back home. Actually...I need to get to my parents if we are done here."

"Yeah, Family, we're done here. Let us know when the product is on the way."

They both rise and shake hands. "Will do," he says.

"Hey, Jeremy, this is Brian Dixon. I need you to come in one last time, then you'll be finished with probation. Come see me Monday morning."

The message ends, and he closes his phone.

God, it's over already? That was fast...but thank God it's done now!

8:00AM comes on Monday, and JJ finds himself in the lobby of Brian's office. Brian opens his door and steps out. "Jeremy, thanks for coming." He follows Brian into the office and sits in the chair across the desk.

"Well, today's your last day," Brian says, smiling. A folder of papers sits directly in front of him. "You've done all that you were supposed to and passed all UAs. I need you to fill out some paperwork, and then you can be on your way." Brian pulls out a few pages from the folder and hands them to JJ.

"Thanks," he replies. He fills out the paperwork as instructed, which doesn't take him long at all. It's the same basic questions required for any type of informational document. He signs the bottom and passes it back across the desk.

Brian takes the papers and smiles. "Well, looks like we are done here." He slides the papers back into the folder. "Good luck, Mr. Jepenski. I hope to never see you again."

He rises from his chair and gives a brief laugh. "Trust me, I don't plan to see you either." They shake hands and say their farewells.

As soon as JJ steps outside, he lets out a deep sigh of relief. He pulls his phone from his pocket and calls George. It rings a few times before George picks up.

"Hey, Bro, meet me at the spot."

"When?" George asks.

"In about an hour."

"Okay, I'll be there."

JJ is sitting at the table of their makeshift lab when George walks in an hour later. Numerous papers fill every inch of the tabletop.

"How did it go?" George asks.

JJ looks up from his spread of papers. "Good...real good. Your big mouth ended up getting Smurf interested in our Bliss product, so he wants to try and sell it. If it does, he will start selling it for us in his area."

George's eyebrows shift upward. "Shit, that's good!"

He nods. "I heard from Mindy and Quick that he moves a lot of weight, too… From how he presents himself, I could see him doing that." He starts shuffling the papers into a pile and continues. "I just finished up my probation today, thank God!"

A smile widens on George's face. "Oh, shit! Time to celebrate! Maybe go out to the club tonight?"

JJ stops shuffling long enough to ponder the suggestion. "You know what…yeah! We haven't been out there for a while!"

"Looks like the club tonight! We'll meet at Club E at 11:00," George answers.

"Sounds good!"

"Pop some powder tonight?"

"I don't like to do our own product," he says.

"Just this once we can!" George says with a smile.

JJ stops him. "Hey, how much did you get made this weekend?"

George takes a moment to think. "I got one complete kilo made…why?"

"Okay, good, because they want ten ounces of powder. How much Bliss do we have?"

George pauses again. "We have...I think, three ounces."

"Alright, get one ounce of Bliss and ten ounces of powder ready for sale. We need to ship it to Quick, and tell them ASAP."

"Okay, I'll have it ready by Wednesday so you can drop it off to Amy."

JJ nods. "Okay." He checks his phone, then shoves the pile of papers into his backpack. "I gotta get going. I'll meet you at the club tonight," he says, grabbing his keys.

"Okay, see you then," George says.

"Honey, I'm home!" he says when he opens the door to his house.

Stacy is sitting on the couch, engrossed in a reality show. Her head turns in his direction when he walks in. "Hey, you! So, you're done with probation now?"

JJ throws his backpack on a nearby chair and plops down next to her. "Yes, I am!" He kisses her. "So, we're going out tonight! Club E, okay?"

She nods. "Yeah, that sounds fun! We haven't been out there for a while."

"Yeah, we're meeting George at 11:00PM."

"Can I invite Amy?"

"Yeah, and tell her to bring Mark," he responds.

When they arrive at Club E later that night, the line is wrapped around the corner. JJ walks up to the front door without hesitation and nods to the bouncer. The guy lets him and Stacy through and shuts the door.

JJ leads them to V.I.P area. George and Amy are there, but no Mark. Amy gives him a big hug.

"Where's Mark?" he asks.

Amy gives a slight shrug. "Well...we haven't really been seeing each other recently."

JJ furrows his brows. "What? Why?"

She shakes her head. "I don't really want to talk about it. It's time to celebrate you getting off paper. So, let's celebrate!" she yells at the top of her lungs.

He pulls out four, clear gel-caps full of ecstasy powder and hands them out. "This is to an excellent night of partying and a long life of friendship!" They raise their glasses and drink down the gel-caps.

They dance until last call and decide to carry the party over to JJ's place. They set up on the patio where they listen to music and wind down. He excuses himself to use the restroom. On his way back to the patio, he finds Amy sitting at the table in the dining room.

"You okay?" he asks.

She looks up absently. "Yeah, I'm fine."

He can hear the sadness in her voice. He pulls up a chair next to her and probes further. "Okay, seriously...you need to stop lying. What's up?"

She looks up at him again. She hesitates before speaking. "Mark is a druggie... He'll never change... He just wants to do drugs, and I hate it." Tears are slowly snaking down her cheeks.

"I thought you liked to party," he says.

She sucks in a labored breath. "I do...but I want more in life than just getting high...and you've been helping me out with money."

He puts a hand on her shoulder. "Amy, you're going to be something in life... Don't let anyone stop you from being you."

A small smile tries to break through on her face. "You really think so, JJ?"

He smiles. "Yes! You're beautiful, funny, smart... You can be whatever you want in life! Fuck Mark! Don't let him bring you down."

She looks at him for a moment. "Thank you, JJ," she replies. She leans in and accepts a hug, but as they start to pull away, she kisses him softly on the lips.

JJ pulls back. "Whoa," he says, stopping her.

"I'm sorry, JJ... I shouldn't have done that." She looks away, but continues to speak. "Sometimes I envy Stacy for having you... I sometimes wish I could have dated you instead of her."

He knows he has to choose his words carefully. "It's okay, Amy...but we are only friends, remember that."

"I know, I know."

"Let's get back out there... This might look suspicious," he says, trying to lighten the tension.

She doesn't look at him, but nods and steps back out on the patio.

George has everything ready on Wednesday as promised. Amy is at the counter when JJ walks into the post office. They say their necessary pleasantries, but there is still definite tension between them.

She gets the package ready for delivery and rings him up.

It is only as he's getting ready to leave that she abruptly apologizes.

His back is turned when she says it. "I'm sorry about the other night," she almost shouts.

He turns and sees her shrink into herself. There is no one else around, but she looks embarrassed.

"It's cool, no worries," he replies, flashing her a smile.

She returns the smile. "Thanks, JJ."

He nods and proceeds back to his car. He gets in and pulls his phone from his pocket. He sends a text to Quick, letting him know the product has been shipped.

Now, we'll just see what happens...

JJ hit me up!

JJ reads the text from Quick and automatically dials his number. It rings twice before Quick answers.

"What's up, Quick?"

"Hold on," Quick responds. JJ can hear shuffling on the other end, but then a different voice speaks.

"Hello?" The voice is deeper and carries more heft.

"Hey, who's this?" he responds.

"It's Smurf, Family."

JJ feels relief wash over him. "Oh, hey! What's up? You good?"

"Yeah! Actually, we wanted to come see you… You free next week?"

JJ is a bit surprised. "Yeah, all week."

"Okay, we will see you Monday or Tuesday, then."

"Alright, yeah, that's cool. I'll see you then," he replies and closes his phone.

Quick and Smurf arrive the following Monday afternoon at his house. They greet one another, and Smurf takes up a seat on the couch. Quick takes the chair next to it. A car show on the Speed Channel is playing on the large sixty-inch-flat-screen television.

"Damn, Family, this is yours?" Smurf asks, looking around.

"Yep, all mine. You like it?"

"Fuck yeah!" Smurf replies.

"Yeah JJ, this place is pretty dope," Quick adds.

JJ sits on the couch by Smurf. "So, what made you guys come all this way to see me?"

Smurf leans forward. "Well, I wanted to drop off that $17,000 I owed you and discuss this Bliss stuff with you... Plus, I wanted to see how you're living, here in Iowa."

"Oh, you sold that already?" he asks.

Smurf smiles as he pulls out a large roll of cash and counts it out for him, making piles of $2,000 on the coffee table. When all $17,000 is in front of them, Smurf puts the remaining wad back into this pocket.

JJ piles all the money together and folds it into his pocket. "So, how was the Bliss?"

"I gave it to a few people, and before I knew it, it was gone," Smurf replies.

JJ raises his eyebrows. "That's good!"

"Yeah, for real, Family! It sold faster than the ecstasy! I would like to buy more Bliss if you got it."

"How much are you wanting to buy?" he asks.

"Shit, Family...half a bird maybe?"

"Half a bird?"

Smurf laughs quickly and corrects himself. "Oh, yeah, sorry...I meant half a kilo."

JJ laughs. "Oh, gotcha! Never heard it called that before."

"How much it going to cost me?" Smurf asks.

"I can do $10,000 for a half a kilo or $15,000 for a full kilo."

"Shit, give me a full kilo of that shit, then!"

JJ nods. "Okay, I'll get on it. You want it right now?"

Smurf shakes his head. "No, ship it."

"Okay, I'll get working on that."

"That's cool," Smurf says. "Hey, also...is your guy available to talk about that business stuff?"

"I'll call him and see." He gets up from the couch and goes into the next room to make the call, leaving Smurf and Quick in the living room. He comes back a couple minutes later. "He said to just meet him at his office."

"When...right now?" Smurf asks.

"Yep."

"Okay, let's go, then!"

They pile into the rental car, and he directs them to the apartment's office. They pull into a spot in front of the office and park.

Smurf scans the area, looking confused. "He's in here?" Smurf asks.

"Yes, he manages this complex also," JJ says, opening his car door.

Chris is filing a small mountain of papers when they enter. "Hey, Chris! These are my friends I was telling you about," JJ says.

Chris extends his hand toward them and they shake. "Nice to meet you guys," Chris says. "So, what brings you all the way out here?"

JJ answers for them. "They are looking for help... Accounting stuff, like what you're helping me with."

Chris looks at Quick and Smurf. "You guys are looking to open a business? What type?" Chris asks.

"No idea," Smurf says. "What do you suggest?"

"Strictly businesses dealing in mostly cash. JJ here owns a party company and a construction company."

Smurf stops him. "First off, how much is this going to cost us?"

"$30,000 year to keep the books straight and to keep you informed about how much you can spend without drawing any unwanted attention," Chris says.

Smurf sits quiet for a moment. "Okay, we'll try it this way. We want a party company."

Chris nods and walks over to a small table in the corner. JJ knows this table well, remembering his appreciation for it the first time he saw

Chris bring it into the office. It had been custom made to look like a small table that was only big enough to fit a lamp, but was actually quite spacious just under the top.

Chris removes the lamp from the table and does a simple maneuver that unlatches the top from the legs.

He removes a folder and re-fastens the top back on the table.

He brings the folder to his desk and starts filling out the paperwork. "What's the name of the company going to be?" Chris asks.

Smurf thinks for a minute. "Let's call it Power Partners Inc."

"Okay," Chris responds, filling in various boxes. He finishes within minutes. "It's all filled out. Now, all you guys need to do is start hosting parties, and I will take care of the rest."

"That's it?" Smurf asks.

Chris nods. "Yup, that's it."

"Hey, Smurf, when my party company holds parties, I'll put your company down to help you move money a little faster," JJ says.

"So, I don't have to worry about the IRS?" Smurf asks.

Chris shakes his head. "Nope. I'll take care of everything. If you have any questions, call me." He hands a business card to both Smurf and Quick. "My cell is on twenty-four hours a day, seven days a week."

"Okay, thanks," Smurf says.

"I'll put in a payment for you now, and you can just pay me when you get back," JJ says to Smurf.

"Yeah, let's do it that way," Smurf agrees.

JJ makes the payment arrangements with Chris, and they leave. They go back to JJ's and head out to the back by the pool. They arrange a few chairs into a circle, and JJ pulls out a small baggie. "You guys want to smoke?" he asks.

They both nod. "You're off papers now, huh?" Smurf asks, laughing.

JJ smiles. "Yup, last week, actually!"

Quick pulls out a blunt wrap from his jacket pocket and quickly rolls a blunt. The guys spend the next few hours passing the blunt and telling stories.

This Smurf dude is pretty cool... Hopefully this is a long-lasting friendship. With our product and his skills, the world is ours for the taking.

"I think it's time to dump the ecstasy and run with the Bliss... We are almost even with amounts of Bliss sold compared to ecstasy," George says.

"I think so, too," JJ agrees.

"JJ, let's put Bliss at 100%... I just can't believe the amounts Smurf is getting! Just months ago, he was trying it out, now he's grabbing a couple kilos every three or four days!" George says with excitement.

"Yeah, he's definitely one of the major distributors, so we must, at any means, keep him 100% satisfied."

George nods. "So, have you talked to our lawyer...Dennis?"

"No, I'm going to call him and make sure we are good to go. The last thing we need is a kink in the chain, you know what I mean, George?"

"I sure do. But hey, I have to get going. Hit me up later, JJ. Don't forget to call Dennis," George says, grabbing his keys from the table.

"Okay, I'll call you and let you know what he says." They bump fists and George leaves.

JJ pulls out his cell and scrolls through his contacts to Dennis Goldman. He presses SEND and waits.

"Hello, this is Dennis," the deep voice says.

"Hey, Dennis. It's JJ."

"How's everything, JJ?"

"Good, very good! I wanted to know if we were all good on this research chemical."

JJ hears papers shuffling on the other end before Dennis continues. "Well, my understanding is that, at this point, it's 100% legal."

"Okay, that's all I needed to know."

"Yep, you're fine," Dennis assures him.

"That's exactly what I wanted to hear."

"Oh, wait, I almost forgot... Do you know anyone by the name of Mark Wilson?" Dennis asks.

Should I say yes...or no?

"Yes, I do...why?"

"He was just recently arrested on drug trafficking charges...ten pounds of hydroponic marijuana. He's in the Story County Jail as we speak."

The blood in JJ's body freezes. "What are his odds of getting out?"

"Very slim... If you see him, that's because he's working." Dennis pauses. "You catch my drift?"

The statement solidifies the ice in his veins. "I understand... Thanks for the heads up." JJ hangs up the phone.

"FUCK! FUCK! FUCK!" he yells, throwing his phone across the room. He puts his hands on his head in frustration.

That motherfucker will ruin us! Ruin me! Now I know why he hasn't been around for a while...FUCK!

He takes a few deep breaths and tries to compose himself. He finds his phone by the wall, and to his amazement it's perfectly fine. He goes to Quick's number and pushes SEND.

"Hey, JJ. What's up?" Quick asks.

"I got a problem; I need your help," he says, trying to mask his worry.

"What is it?"

JJ sits down in the chair. "I'll tell you when you get here. I'll keep you posted on exactly what is going on when you get here, but get here soon. This is very important to everyone... Do you understand?"

Quick doesn't ask any questions. "Yeah, I do, JJ. We'll be there soon."

He disconnects the call and tosses his phone on the table. He takes one last deep breath as he leans back in his chair.

Goodbye, Mark, you motherfucker!

TANYA

"Hey, Papi, you needed to talk to me?" she says as she closes the office door behind her.

Papi looks up from a stack of papers. "Yeah, thanks for meeting me down here at the restaurant."

"No problem... What's up?" she asks.

"Well, the Guzmans called for a meeting between families."

She looks at him, somewhat confused. "For what reason?"

"Honestly, I'm not 100% sure... I just know it has something to do with territory issues."

This ignites her anger. "So they call a meeting for it? God! These fuckers are doing all this political shit over land? We should just take it all and leave them high and dry!"

Papi sighs. "Yeah, but that would start a war."

She's fuming. "So what? I prefer that whole family dead! Especially after what they did to my dad and my brother!"

Papi tries to interrupt. "No, you don't--"

She cuts him off. "I don't what, Papi? Don't know?" Her words are heated, but she stops for a moment before continuing. "Can I ask you a serious question? Do you even care that your brother, MY FATHER, was murdered by these punks that call themselves a family?"

Now, Papi's anger flares. "Yes, I care Tanya! What are you trying to say?"

"I'm not saying anything…but as I look at you, I don't see the same man I appointed to be the face of this family a few years ago…after my father's death."

"You saying I'm soft?" he shouts.

"No!" she shoots back. "You just changed."

"I'm not the one changing; you are!"

She lets out a slight laugh in disagreement. "Oh, yeah? This is good… Flatter me… How have I changed?"

"Ever since you've been hanging out with that black boy, your attitude has changed. Shoot first; ask questions later. It's going to ruin this family!"

"Why do you say that…because I want to wipe out the Guzman family?"

"Yes, Tanya. You and I both know our family is large and in more places than just Chicago. We make billions of dollars a year in both legal and illegal business. A war with this little, shit family will do nothing but stir up attention and drama for our family." Papi takes a second to compose himself, taking a deep breath. "Your dad, God rest his soul, was a smart man. He thought about the family and their wellbeing above all things. You learned a lot from him, but you're not using all that he taught you. There's always a time and a place for personal vendettas, and this is not it."

Tears form in her eyes. "What do we do, then?"

"We go meet with them...discuss the problem and fix it."

Tanya takes a deep breath. "Fine. When is this meeting?"

"Tonight...8:00 at Las Margaritas on Cicero."

"Fine!" she barks. "Pick me up around 7:30 at the condo." She turns and storms towards the door.

"I'll be there," Papi says as she walks through the door. He knows she can't hear him. Her senses are blinded by rage.

Tanya's in the lobby, waiting impatiently. She just wants to get this over with. Her phone vibrates from inside her purse. She digs it out and opens it.

"Hey, I'm outside," Papi says. She doesn't say anything. She just closes the phone and meets him in the car.

The ride to the restaurant is quiet, but soon enough they're in the parking lot and headed through the front door. A waitress appears from the back, notices Papi, and approaches. "This way, Sir," she says. They follow her upstairs to a private dining area on the second floor. There are banquet-like rooms with plain, light-brown walls. Marco Guzman and one other man are sitting at a table in the corner.

"Welcome, sit down," Marco says in broken English.

Darkness fills Tanya as she stares down her father's killer.

I want to just shoot his ass in the head.

She puts on a fake smile and greets him. "Hello Marco," she says.

Goodbye Marco.

She's lost in fantasy, watching Marco's head explode as she empties a clip.

"Tanya," Papi says, nudging her back to reality. "Pay attention," he whispers.

Marco sits down and begins speaking. "I called this meeting because of a problem we're having with territory."

They sit down across from him. "What's the problem?" Papi asks.

"We came to an agreement on territory lines throughout the city...

Recently, we've noticed a lot of your product ending up in our neighborhoods."

Papi readjusts in his seat. "Are you saying our people are selling on your land?"

"No, but it's the people you're selling to."

"Are you serious?" Tanya says in an angry voice. "You want us to control who those people sell to, as well?"

"You're stealing our business."

"We are selling shit!" she yells.

"Calm down, Tanya," Papi says.

Tanya's thoughts are flooded with images of her brother and father's dead bodies. Her anger explodes.

"I won't calm down, Papi!"

Papi looks to Marco. "I apologize, Marco... She's been a little edgy lately."

Marco puts his hand up. "Don't apologize, Papi."

Tanya begins to taunt Marco. "I just realized you're a fucking baby! Wahhh, wahhh!" She wipes away at her fake tears.

"Tanya!" Papi yells.

Tanya turns to Papi. "No, Papi, you just listen." She turns back to Marco. "Marco, you act like you're a big drug lord, but yet you cry over shit we have no control of... I think it might be time for you to retire. You're getting soft."

"I will show you soft, bitch!" Marco says as he reaches for his gun.

She beats him to it and pulls out a long, .45 caliber pistol, aiming it at his head. "Now, you listen to me, Marco. You stay out of my way, and I'll stay out of yours. I'll stop the sale of product in your areas, but once it leaves my hands, I no longer have any part of it." She stares at him hard. "And don't think for one fucking minute I'm soft, because the next time we cross paths, we won't both be leaving...you feel me?"

Marco says nothing.

"Papi, get up... This meeting is over," she says, lowering her gun. She storms out of the room, and Papi quickly follows.

He catches up with her at the front door. "I can't believe you, Tanya!" Papi shouts. "Your father would never do anything like that!"

She keeps her fast pace. "Well, Papi, I'm not my father. That man is a coward! Crying about product in his territory...like we have control of that! I don't get paid to babysit, and if that's what I'm doing, why am I selling drugs again?"

They both stop at rear of the car. "You could have just started a war!" Papi yells.

She laughs lightly. "You and I both know we would kill his family and take everything...and I think that little puke's head would look good in my living room."

He eyes her for a moment, then smiles. "You're crazy," Papi says as he begins to laugh.

She smiles. "Tell me something I don't know."

He drives her home, and little more is said. He drops her off at the front door and drives away.

Within minutes, Smurf picks her up and drives back to his place.

"What's up, Ma?" he asks as they walk through the front door. She sits in the middle of the couch. "Something's wrong...I can tell," he continues.

"I'm okay, I'm fine," she responds.

"Stop lying. I can see it in your eyes... There is a lot of sadness and anger in there."

Tears gather in her eyes, and one spills over, rolling down her cheek. "Smurf?"

"Yeah?" he replies, wiping the lonely tear away.

"Have you ever wanted something so badly...but you knew if you got it, it could cause great pain to yourself and others?"

"Honestly, it's human nature to want what you can't have." Her phone rings, and she pulls it from her purse. "Who is that?" he asks.

"Oh, it's Mindy... Let me see what she wants." She lifts the phone up to her ear. "Hello?" Smurf watches her brows furrow. Her mood changes, signaling him that this is one of those calls you don't want to get.

"When did it happen?" she asks. Sadness fills her voice. "Is he okay?" She stays quiet for a moment. "Yeah...okay, I'll be down there soon." She hangs up and frantically puts the cell back in her purse.

There is a hint of urgency, but she looks lost.

"What happened?" Smurf asks.

Tanya looks at him, dazed. "Quick got shot."

His eyes widen. "He good?" he asks.

She shakes off her stupor. "Yeah, it hit him in the shoulder."

"We going to see him?"

"Yes...he needs to tell us something, I guess. At least, that is what Mindy told me."

"Right, let's go," he replies, reaching for his keys.

They arrive at the hospital and find Mindy standing out in the hallway.

"Where is he?" Tanya asks.

Mindy doesn't say anything. She just points to the room across the hall.

They follow her finger and open the door. Quick is in bed, bandaged up. Multiple monitors beep around him. The blinds are shut, and the lights are mostly dimmed, but he's awake.

Tanya runs up to him. "Quick!" she says frantically. "What happened?"

Smurf tries to keep it cool. "What up, cuz? How are you holding up?"

Quick smiles. "Hey, Tanya. Hey, Smurf." He doesn't wait for them to ask any more questions. "I was cruising down the block to some spots to pick up money, and I stopped at a red light with my window down. I was listening to some music, and then I notice all these niggas come out of everywhere, like fucking bugs...and start busting my car. So, I try to take off, and I see this other nigga come from around the corner liquor store and noticed he was heading towards the car."

"He say anything?" she asks.

"He said something about staying out of his hood... Then I saw him pull his gun. I was in the middle of the intersection when he shot me...at first I thought he missed, but then I felt the heat coming from my shoulder as I sped away. I lost consciousness and wrecked into a pole."

"What did this guy look like?" she probes. Quick describes a young, black male in his late twenties, with a facial description that sounds almost like Smoke Jr.

He isn't out yet...is he?

"We'll get this figured out," Smurf says to him.

"Yeah, I'll put a hole in the niggas head," Tanya says with a laugh.

"Hey, I need to make a call. I'll be back," Smurf says before exiting the room.

He returns ten minutes later and only steps in the doorway. "Hey, Tanya, can I talk to you alone?"

She looks up. "Yeah." She turns back to Quick. "We'll be right back," she says, tapping his leg.

She meets Smurf in the hallway, and he closes the door behind her. "What's going on?" she asks.

"I think it was Smoke Jr."

"You mean the person who shot Quick?" she asks.

Smurf nods. "Yeah...I made some calls and found out his case didn't stick... He's out."

Tanya's face goes hard. "Are you sure?"

"Yeah. He described him perfectly... I know it's him...but why would he shoot him? And why would he tell him to stay out of his neighborhood?"

Fucking Marco Guzman... I bet he's working for him.

It takes almost a full minute for Tanya to respond. "I'm not sure."

She stays with Quick through the night and wakes up early. The hospital cots they provide are about as comfortable as the floor. Quick is still asleep. She slowly gets up, grabs her purse and steps out into the hall. She closes the door and grabs her phone out of her purse. Her fingers punch in familiar numbers, and she waits.

"Hello?" Papi answers.

She doesn't greet him. "We need to talk; it's important. Meet me at the restaurant."

Papi doesn't ask questions. "Okay, I'll be there forty-five minutes."

He arrives exactly forty-five minutes later. They are the only two at the restaurant, but that's to be expected at this time.

"What's so important?" Papi asks, pulling up a chair across from her.

"Alex was shot yesterday," she says.

Papi's eyes grow. "What? When?"

She gives a slight shrug. "Sometime after our meeting."

"He's okay?" Papi asks, looking hopeful.

"Yeah, they hit him in the shoulder...but I think the guy works for Marco."

Papi's worry turns to anger. "I knew that shit would kick off some drama... I told you, Tanya!" he yells.

"Well, Uncle, I'm not for sure, but Smurf thinks it's a man named Smoke Jr. I need you to see if this guy works for Marco."

He stares at her, and then sighs deeply. "I'll see what I can do. I should know by the end of the day. Do me a favor... Hang low for a while...until we get this figured out, okay?"

"Okay, Papi. As soon as you hear something, let me know."

"I will." The worry is back on his face. "Now, get home."

She nods, and then leaves.

At home, she manages to sleep for a few hours. With her nerves and constant thoughts, the sleep isn't good.

Hell, it's better than nothing.

She stretches and decides on a shower. She stands under the hot spray, wishing the events from the past forty-eight hours could wash away as easily as dirt and sweat.

She's finishing up getting dressed when her phone rings. It's Papi. "Hey, I'll be over in an hour. I got something." The line goes silent.

Tanya's curiosity is peaked. She is waiting for him at the door when he arrives an hour later.

"What did you find out?" she asks as they walk into the living room.

He sits in an older recliner next to the couch. "I found out that this Smoke guy does indeed work for Marco. He is a mid-level distributor...but I also found out that 'soft' shit you said must have touched a nerve. He put out a hit on any big-wig dealer of ours caught on of his territory."

This information is fuel for her fire. "Oh, so he wants to play like that, huh?"

Papi shrugs. "I guess."

"Well, let's run his ass out of business! Find out who his supplier is…fuck up shipments. No product, no money, no family. We'll get ahold of our government contacts and start pressing them…let them know any money or drugs we take from the Marco, we'll give them half the street value in cash on the product or half the cash is theirs if they get the money."

Papi looks skeptical. "Seriously?"

"Yes," she says with definite conviction. "First, we kill the business, steal the clients and then watch him squirm. Then we kill them…but leave Marco for me. I will personally kill his ass!"

Papi takes a deep breath and nods. "Alright."

Her fire is in full flame. "If this motherfucker wants a war, then it's a war we'll give him."

JJ

It's been hours, but he only has one more to go. He grabs his phone from the cup holder and calls George.

"Hey, George, can you meet me at the house in like an hour? I need to talk to you."

"Yeah, I can...everything okay?" George asks.

"Yeah, I'll tell you what's up when you get here. Cool?"

"Yeah, that's fine. See you in about an hour," George replies.

They arrive at his house at almost the same time an hour later.

"Hey! Just getting back?" George asks, stepping out of his car.

JJ's already out of his car, but opens the back door to grab his bag. "No, I had to run to the store first. Come on in," he replies.

He unlocks the door and automatically drops his bag on the table upon walking into the kitchen.

"So, how was Chicago?" George asks.

JJ turns around to face him. "That's what I wanted to talk to you about."

George furrows his eyebrows. "Something wrong?" George asks, choosing a spot on the loveseat in the living room.

"How would you like to live in Chicago?" he asks.

This question catches George off guard. He takes a few seconds before uttering a single word.

"What?" George laughs nervously.

"No, seriously, George. We were offered a job in Chicago!"

George stops laughing. "Doing what?"

JJ smiles. "Making Bliss. And mad amounts of it!"

George takes another few moments to take in this new information. "I don't know, JJ..."

"Stop that shit, George! Mindy's in Chicago... If we move there, we can be whoever we want to be! No more running around to drop-offs and pickups. We make it for one person only *and* make one hundred times more than what we are now."

"What about our houses? The businesses? Our lives here?" George asks.

"Don't you want to leave this town and make some real money?" He pauses for emphasis. "I thought you said you're always in."

"I am JJ, but-- "

He cuts him off. "But nothing. If you're in, then we're leaving soon. I'm just waiting on a call. Don't worry about the businesses; we'll sell them or give them to someone to run for us, and we'll collect a percentage every month."

George eyes him, taking everything into consideration. "You know what you're doing, so I trust your decisions. What has Stacy said about all this?"

He looks away. "I haven't told her about it."

"What!" George exclaims.

"I'm waiting for the right time!" he shoots back.

"You better do it soon."

He exhales. "I know, I know... I will."

Almost as if on cue, Stacy enters through the garage entrance. "Helloooo, I'm home!" she yells.

George's eyes widen, and his head shoots to JJ. "Shit! Here's your chance, JJ! I'll leave and let you guys talk."

Stacy enters the room. "What are you guys doing?"

"Hi, Stacy," George replies.

"Hi, Honey," JJ says. "George was just getting ready to leave."

"No, stay for a while!" Stacy says.

George hesitates for a moment, trying to think up a quick excuse. "I would, but I have to get some stuff done." George looks to JJ. "JJ, call me later." Then to Stacy. "Stacy, always a pleasure."

They both say goodbye as George leaves by the front door. Stacy turns back to JJ. "How was Chicago?" she asks.

"Good, good." He is unsure how to begin this conversation. "Hey, Honey, sit down for second," he says, indicating the spot next to him.

"O...kay...?" she says, confused. "Is something wrong?"

He shakes his head. "No, I need to ask you something."

"What is it?"

He takes a deep breath and exhales through his nose. "If I was to move to Chicago, would you come?"

Her head bobs back. "What? When? Why?"

"I don't know...soon though," he replies.

"Seriously? You know I got half a year left of school... I can't just leave." He can see her visibly filing this information away. "Why do you want to move so badly?"

"I got offered a job."

She waits. "Doing...?"

A grin appears across his face.

Her expression instantly changes. "Are you serious, JJ? You're chasing a dope man's dream!" she shouts. She is anything BUT happy.

"I was offered a job making one hundred times more than I do now...and I have to do less," he tries explaining.

"I can't believe you!" she yells.

"What you do you mean?"

"Wanting to move to be a drug dealer? You're a college kid, JJ!"

He puts his hands up in defense. "Stacy, a college kid didn't buy you this house, the car you're driving or the fancy clothes and purses you own."

"I don't care about that shit! Take it back!"

"I wanted--"

She doesn't give him a chance to speak. "You're getting too deep into this... You're going to end up in prison or dead!"

The comment sparks his anger. "Thanks for being so positive!" he yells back at her.

"I'm just stating facts, JJ!" She begins to cry, laying her head in her hands.

He waits a few awkward moments. "I'm guessing that's a no," he says.

She looks up at him, her makeup smeared. "I won't watch you

destroy yourself. I love you too much to just sit back."

He clenches his jaw. "Fine, then! I'll go to Chicago alone!" he yells. He picks up the lamp on the end table and throws it against the wall. He breathes hard, letting the rage and frustration burn. "You know what, Stacy? I don't want any of this shit! The house, the car...it's all yours, all for free! My gift to you! Consider it an early graduation present!" He turns toward the door.

"Don't go, JJ! Please don't go!" she pleads.

Her turns to her again. "I have nothing, Stacy, NOTHING. Mark fucked that up for me, and because of him, I'm doing what I love."

"But it's on the grey side of the law," she says through swollen eyes.

He hates seeing her like this. Her tears become the water to quench the fire in him, and he softens. "I love you, Stacy. You're going to be great in life, I know it...but I got to do this for me."

He watches the corners of her mouth pull down. "I love you too, JJ," she says. They sit in awkward silence. "So this is it?... I was hoping it wasn't over yet."

He pulls her to him and holds her. "We just want different things in life."

The moment is over quickly. His phone rings, and he checks it. "Hold on one second," he says to Stacy. "It's Dennis; I have to take this."

He flips his phone open.

"Hello, JJ," the deep voice says.

"Hey, Dennis, how are you?"

"I'm fine. I'm calling to let you know that the individual is out... Just remember what I said before."

Great, just what I need.

"Okay, thanks, Dennis, for the heads up."

"Just doing my job. Oh...looks like I got another call. If I hear anything else, I'll let you know," Dennis says.

"Okay, thanks again," he says, then closes his phone.

Fuck, Mark's out...

"What was that about?" Stacy asks.

"Nothing. Dennis was just calling to check up on me."

She eyes him. "Are you sure?" she asks.

"Yeah, but enough about that. I'll get all the paperwork set up tomorrow for the house and car... All you'll need to do is sign. I'll cover all the costs to switch the names. Just go see Chris Fleming, and he'll take care of you."

Stacy just nods as more tears spill from her eyes.

"Don't worry," he says. "I'll keep my eye on you... from a distance. I promise."

"Do you?" she asks.

"I swear. If you need a little bit of money, just talk to Chris, okay?"

"Okay," she responds, the corners of her lips dropping again.

"But, hey, I got to run. I'll be back later, okay?"

"Okay, I guess," she says sadly.

He kisses her softly on the lips, wiping tears from her eyes, and leaves. His first priority is seeing Chris.

As he's driving, he pulls out his phone and punches in numbers without looking. Amy answers on the second ring.

"Hello?" she says.

"You busy?"

"For about an hour or two...why?"

He clears his throat. "No reason, just need to talk. Give me a call when you're done, and I'll come pick you up, okay?"

"Okay, I'll call you in a bit," she replies.

He pulls into the apartment parking lot, just as the conversation ends. He walks in and sits in the chair across from Chris.

"What's going on?" Chris asks.

"Well, Chris, I came over here to talk to you because George and I are moving."

Chris raises his eyebrows. "Oh yeah? Where?"

"We're moving to Chicago, but the businesses, the houses, the cars... I need to get them signed over into other names."

"Okay, not a problem. What goes where?" Chris asks, pulling out a legal pad and a ball point pen.

The house I share with Stacy and the other SL500 need to go to Stacy for a sale price of $1000."

He watches Chris jot notes with a quick hand. "Okay...the other houses?"

"George's house goes to a girl named Amy. She also gets the party company and my SL500."

"Same price?" Chris asks.

"Yeah."

"Okay." More furious scribbles. "And the last house...the other house Stacy doesn't know about?"

"It's yours, Chris. So is the construction company, free and clear. All I ask is that you send 10% of what you make each month to me and George. And if Stacy or Amy need money, you give them some as well."

Chris leans back in his chair. "Why are you doing this?"

"It's time to start fresh. Start over new in a new city. Stacy and Amy will be coming to sign the stuff into their names. Whatever the cost, take my money and pay for it."

"Okay, I'll do that. Are you ever coming back?"

He shrugs. "I might, but I need you to be my eyes and ears down here."

"Alright, anything, JJ. You've given so much to me," Chris says.

"Just keep an eye on Stacy and Amy for me. If they start doing any stupid shit, let me know...got it?"

"I got it...anything stupid, I'll call you."

JJ nods. "Okay, I'm going to get going. Get that paperwork ready for tomorrow."

"Yes, Sir," Chris says, giving a salute.

JJ laughs. "Stop that stuff, Chris."

"Okay, sorry, JJ!" With that, he leaves the office.

He gets into his car and takes a few deep, relaxing breaths. He starts up his SL500 Mercedes Roadster and pulls out his phone. He types his message to Quick and presses SEND before leaving the parking lot.

That potential just became a problem.

He drives around town for a while, waiting for Amy to call back. He's almost through campus when his phone rings.

"Hello?" he answers.

"Hey, JJ, just calling you back from earlier," Amy says.

"Where are you at?" he asks.

"I'm down on Beach Street by the gym. Where are you at?"

"I'm on Lincoln Way. I'll come to you... I'll be there in five minutes." He closes his phone.

He pulls into the gym parking lot and is greeted by a sea of college kids. He doesn't have to wait long before he sees Amy, wearing a sports bra and spandex shorts. Their eyes meet and she jogs to his car.

"What's up?" she asks as she gets into the car.

"Nothing," he replies. He tries averting his gaze, but he keeps looking back at her partially-clothed body.

"What are you looking at?" she asks, smiling.

JJ utters a nervous laugh. "Sorry...first time seeing you with so little clothes on. I can see why Mark's been so interested for so long," he replies, flashing a smile of his own.

"Hey, now," she says flirtatiously, hitting his arm.

They continue to drive until he finds an empty parking lot near a few empty baseball fields. He parks the car and turns to her. "The reason why I needed to talk to you is to tell you to go visit this guy tomorrow." He hands her Chris' business card.

"About what?" she asks.

"I need your signature for some stuff."

"What stuff?"

"Damn, what's with all the questions?" he asks, slightly annoyed.

"I just want to know what I'm signing for, that's all," she says in defense.

"I put the L.K.E party company in your name. I'm giving it to you."

Shock overtakes her features. "What? Really? Why?"

"That's not all," he continues. "You get a house, also. And this car, too."

Her eyes somehow manage to open wider, and her mouth nearly drops to the floor. It takes her a minute before she finds any words.

"What's the catch?" she asks.

"No catch, Amy. You're a good girl, and for all the stuff you did for me, I figured you deserved this. All I ask is that you stay away from drugs and Mark. He is a bad influence on you."

"I will."

He looks more intently at her, emphasizing the seriousness of his words. "Promise me you will," he says.

"I promise I will... Why are you doing this?"

"I'm moving away."

Shock is replaced by sudden curiosity on Amy's face. "Are you coming back?"

"Probably not, but don't think I don't have eyes and ears keeping track of you."

Amy smiles. "Where you going?"

"I'm going back to Chicago...but if anyone asks, you don't know, okay?"

"Okay, I don't know where you went."

"Good girl," he replies as he rubs her head.

"What about Stacy?" she asks.

He breathes deep. "She's finishing school... We are just heading in two different directions. She's taking our house and her car, too. It was my early graduation present to her."

There's a long silence before Amy finally speaks. "I can't believe you're leaving."

He shrugs. "It's time to go back home."

"Well since you and-- "

He stops her midsentence by placing his lips against hers. He kisses her deeply and pulls away.

"Only one time couldn't hurt, right?" he says.

She just smiles and shakes her head. They come together again, first with passionate kisses, and then he works his way over to her ear, nibbling on the lobe.

"Damn, this car is small," he says as he tries to adjust his chair. She climbs on top of him and pulls her sports bra off and tosses it to the passenger side floor. He starts licking and sucking her nipples.

She lets off a soft moan as she rubs her fingers through his hair.

She gets in the passenger seat and pulls off her shorts and unzips his pants, then unbuttons them and pulls them towards the pedals. She takes his shaft in her hand and starts slowly moving her hand up and down. She starts lightly kissing the tip, and then slowly swallows his dick until he's fully down her throat. She raises her ass in the air for a better angle, and he starts to lightly finger her wet pussy. Each time she sucks he pumps his fingers into her.

"You got a condom?" she asks.

"I don't," he responds.

"Shit...fuck it, I can't wait," she says. She gets back on top, straddling him. She slowly lowers herself onto him, pushing the head of his dick into her. As she starts riding him, she starts moaning loudly. The sensations push her towards climax.

She tries to grab onto something and ends up accidentally hitting the car horn. They both start to laugh, but the pumping doesn't cease. He starts sucking on her tits as his dick goes deeper and deeper into her.

"Fuck, Amy, I didn't know your sex was this good!" he moans.

She just smiles, gripping his shoulders as she climbs closer to climax. He can feel her tighten around him, and he increases his pumps. It's like an explosion when she comes all over him.

"Oh shit," she moans. She takes his hand and smacks her ass. "Fuck me, JJ," she moans, riding him slower.

He can feel it coming. "Where do want me to come?" he groans.

"All over me."

He pumps her slow, feeling inside her. The sensations intensify, and he's on the edge now. He pulls out and comes all over her stomach.

She takes him in her hand and squeezes every drop out of him. "God, JJ, I hate you... I want this dick!"

"Sorry, Amy, one-time thing...unless you find me in Chicago," he says, smiling.

"I know, I know," she moans as she wipes herself, off then him, She kisses him again. "Thank you, JJ, for everything."

"No, Amy, thank you. We better get back so you can go change."

"Yeah," she begins to laugh. "You're right, I need to change and take a shower," she says as she sits down in the passenger seat to finish getting dressed.

He drops her back off at the gym. "Don't forget to contact Chris," he says. They kiss one last time before he takes off back towards his house. On his way, he calls George.

"Hey, took care of everything. Now, we just wait."

"Okay, just let me know when," George says.

"Okay, I will."

"But I'll talk to you later. Mindy is on the other line," George replies.

"Oh, my bad!" he responds.

"It's all good! We'll talk later. See you," George responds and hangs up.

When he gets home, he hops in the shower. The events of the day wash through his mind like the water down his back...the fight with Stacy, the sex with Amy, the move to Chicago. It's a lot to take in one day.

After finishing his shower, he finds Stacy asleep in their bed. She looks so peaceful. All the things she told him keep haunting his memories. He pulls up the blanket, tucking her in, and kisses her softly on the forehead.

He heads to the living room and plops down on the couch. He pulls up a movie on TV. Anything to take his mind off reality. His phone beeps next to him, and he opens his phone. It's a text from Quick.

It's handled

He closes his phone and tosses it on the couch next to him. "Good,"

he says to himself.

MINDY

"Mindy!" Tanya yells from the living room of the condo.

"Yeah, Tanya?" she responds.

"Come here, I need to talk to you!"

"Okay! Hold on one second!" Not even a minute passes before she meets her cousin in the kitchen. "What's up?" she says, grabbing a soda from the refrigerator.

"Mindy, I need you to do something for the family."

"What is it?" The cracking sound of the pop can echoes through the kitchen.

"I need you to go to Iowa and take care of a problem. His name is Mark Wilson... He could really hurt this family, and we need to stop any chance of that at all costs."

"Alright. Do you have a picture?" Mindy asks.

Tanya reaches in her purse and pulls out a folded piece of paper. She hands it to Mindy. "This is a copy of Mark's driver's license picture– it's the picture we have from our government source, as is the address. This needs to look like an accident, so I'll leave it up to your imagination."

Mindy studies the picture, taking mental notes.

Damn, this boy must have really fucked up...

"When does this need to be done?" she asks.

"Immediately."

"Alright, I'll get ready and leave today."

"Take care of this and just stay with George for the night...but get in, get out, and get back here ASAP."

Mindy nods. "Okay, I will. Anything else?"

"Good luck," Tanya says. She pulls Mindy in for a hug, and then they part ways.

Mindy packs a bag and makes arrangements for a rental car. After five hours of driving, she calls George.

"Hi, Honey," he answers.

"Hey, what are you doing?"

"Nothing too much, how about you?"

"I'm actually heading to Omaha, and I wanted to stop by for the night."

"Really?" George says with excitement. "Where are you at now?"

"Well, I'm on highway thirty, about an hour outside of Ames."

"Really? So, you'll be here in about an hour then?"

"Yeah, I should be."

"Okay, well, call when you pass the I-35 North exit, and I'll tell you where to meet me, okay?"

"Okay, Honey. See you soon," she says. The call ends. She looks at the picture of Mark on the dashboard, constantly studying it.

When she gets to the designated exit, she calls George. He gives her directions to Best Buy and tells her he'll meet her there. "I'll be in a black Lexus," he says before he disconnects.

She finds the Best Buy and pulls into the partially empty parking lot. She finds a spot near the exit, away from other cars. She scans the area, looking for a black Lexus. She spots a slow-moving black Lexus coming toward her with two people inside. As it pulls up, she sees George driving. She gets out of the car to stretch, and he gets out of his car.

"Hey, you," he says as he gives her a big hug and a kiss.

"Hey," she replies. She looks into his car and sees another white male. "Who's your friend?"

"Oh, sorry, that's my friend, Mark. Mark, this is Mindy," George says through the open window to Mark.

She leans to get a good look at him.

Shit, that's him! That's Mark!

She puts on a fake smile. "Hi, Mark. Nice to meet you." Mark puts his hand up and gives a small nod.

"So, how long are you in town for?" George asks.

"Oh, just tonight. I gotta leave tomorrow," she replies.

"Well, come on. Follow us back to my place," he says as he gets in his car. She does the same and follows him to his nice, two-story home on the north side of town.

"Nice to see my second home," she says and laughs when she enters.

"I know, right? But I'll be leaving it soon to move to Chicago," George says, but stops. "I mean…you knew JJ and I are moving there soon, didn't you?" She plays it off like she hadn't a clue, raising her eyebrows and shrugging. George quickly changes the subject. "So, Mindy, since you're in town, what you want to do tonight?"

"I want to party at the club!" she says.

"Well, we can hit up Club E and get some bottles. Sound good?"

Mindy nods. "Yeah, that sounds like fun!" She turns to Mark. "Are you going to come, Mark? You should! It will be fun!"

"Sure, I haven't been out for a while," Mark replies.

"Okay, then, it's settled!" George says. "Club E tonight at, let's say….11:00PM?"

Mark and Mindy nod in agreement.

"Hey, George, I need to get going. Can you give me a ride home?" Mark asks.

"Yeah, Mindy and I can drop you off."

In the car, all Mindy can think about is her task at hand. She brainstorms different scenarios, playing and replaying them over in her mind. Everything has to be perfect. Not one slip-up. By the time they drop Mark off, Mindy already knows what she's going to do.

George pulls into their reserved parking spot at Club E a little before 11:00PM. Just one of the many perks of owning a party business.

Inside, they maneuver through the crowded dance floor to the V.I.P table closest to the DJ booth.

They order two bottles and wait for Mark to arrive. It doesn't take long before Mindy spots him.

"Sorry I'm late!" he yells over the loud bass.

George shakes his head and hands him a full glass of vodka and orange juice. "Here, drink up!"

Mindy watches Mark. She's studied his picture enough, now she has to study his habits in the short time she has. No slip-ups.

At around 1:00 in the morning, Mark has found himself a red-haired beauty. She's petite and looks to be in her mid-twenties. She watches as he pulls the girl in their direction, more than likely to keep the girl liquored up. The pair doesn't even make it to the table before they're lost in an alcohol-induced make out session.

Mindy sees this opportunity and puts her plan into action. Everyone around her is too far into the music or too busy grinding to notice her exploits. Even George is away for the moment. She pulls a small plastic tube from her purse and dumps some white powder into Mark's drink. With one hand, she picks up the glass and swivels it from side to side, further mixing the substance. With the other, she puts the tube back into her purse.

She watches as George pushes his way through the crowd. He sees Mark entangled with the redhead and laughs. He slides up beside her and whispers in her ear, "Looks like he caught one."

She smiles and laughs with him, casually eyeing the drink.

Mark and the redhead stop kissing. and Mark pulls her over to their table. "Guys, this is Jessica, Jessica, this is George and Mindy."

They nod and say their hellos. Mindy still eyes the drink, mentally urging Mark to drink it.

Mark picks up the glass. "Here, Jessica, drink this." Mindy's heart momentarily stops.

FUCK! DON'T DRINK IT!

She stays motionless as Jessica guzzles down the drink, not even leaving a drop. This isn't how this was supposed to happen.

George can see the distress Mindy's in. He leans in closer. "Hey, Mindy, you okay?"

She shakes her head. "No, I have a terrible headache... Can we leave yet?"

"Yeah, we can leave," George replies. He turns to Mark and nudges his shoulder. "Hey, Mark, we're going to leave. Mindy has a bad headache."

"Okay George, I'll see you guys later. Hope you get better, Mindy," Mark says.

She just smiles and nods. All she can think about is that poor, innocent girl. Dead because of her.

The thought tears at her insides.

I've never had a civilian casualty before.

Back at the house, she feels her guilt melting away with reality. It's just her and George now.

"I need to shower," she says in a sexy voice. George smiles and leads her to the bathroom.

They slowly undress each other and begin kissing. She gets into the shower grabs his hand, pulling him in with her. The spray of hot water beats down on them as they continue to kiss and touch each other. He kisses her neck and lets his hands wander, feeling and caressing her wet body.

She lets off a moan as she glides her hands down his back and onto his firm ass. He slowly starts to kiss his way to her tits, then begins licking and sucking on each nipple. She continues to run her fingers through his hair, pushing his head down between her legs.

"Eat my pussy," she moans.

He lifts one of her legs up and sets it on his shoulder. He slowly pulls her lips apart and reveals her swollen, pink clit. He begins to lick it with the tip of his tongue. As he continues to lick her swollen clit, he slowly slips his middle finger into her and rubs softly on her G-spot.

"Oh God!" she moans. Her hips gyrate to the rhythm of his tongue. The sensations he's creating inside of her send rushes through her body. "Fuck me... I want to feel you inside of me," she moans.

She grabs him by the hair and tugs him upwards. He stands, and she turns to the wall. She pulls her ass cheeks apart, showing him the way. He lets off a deep moan as the head of his hard dick slides into her.

As he goes deeper, she grabs onto the shower wall. "Right there," she moans as he starts to fill her with deep, penetrating thrusts. He pulls her by her hair, kissing her neck. He thrusts himself deeper into her. The sensation is almost too much to bear.

Her legs begin to shake. "Oh my God, George! Oh my God!" Her body explodes in rushes as she reaches climax. "I'm coming... I'm coming!" she screams.

He can feel her orgasm cover his dick. He continues to pump her with deep thrusts. "I'm about to come," he moans. She pulls him out and begins sucking him off. His toes curl up as he lets off a deep moan and orgasms into her mouth.

She continues to suck on the tip, getting every last drop out of him.

"Oh shit," he moans as he watches her spit his semen down the drain.

She wakes up before George. The events of last night did not go according to plan, so now it's time for plan B. She just has to come up with it.

I need a new car and a hotel room for starters.

She's in the kitchen writing down numerous phone numbers when she hears George. He walks into the kitchen in his boxers, his hair tangled in all directions. Through a sleepy mist, he rubs an eye.

"Why're you up so early? Come back to bed."

She smiles at his sleepy state and shakes her head. "I would, but I need to get going."

"Already?" he asks, yawning.

"Yeah, I'm sorry, Honey. But just think...when you get to Chicago, we'll be together all the time!" She flashes him a big smile and walks to him. She kisses him on the cheek and wraps her arms around his shoulders.

"I guess," he says in a sad voice.

She gives him a soft, passionate kiss. "You know I love you, right?" she whispers.

"I love you too, Mindy. I just wish we could have spent more time together."

"Soon, George, very soon."

At the car company, she switches the car she came in for a black Ford Focus. She finds a Super 8 by the highway and books a room for a couple nights. After getting everything situated, she calls Tanya.

"Hello?" Tanya answers.

"Hey, Cousin."

"You on your way back?" Tanya asks.

"No, not yet."

"When, then?"

"There was a problem, but it's all under control... Probably tomorrow."

"Well, get it taken care of and get back here ASAP!"

"I will let you know when it's done," she assures Tanya.

"Okay, if you need me just call."

"Okay, Tanya. Talk to you later." She ends the call.

She reaches for her purse, shuffling the contents around until she finds the small tube from the previous night. Anger builds inside her.

That poor girl never had a chance…

She goes into the bathroom and flushes the tube down the toilet. She goes back to her luggage and pulls out a small .25 caliber pistol and a loaded clip.

I'm not leaving 'til he's dead.

She still has Mark's address in her purse. She waits a few hours, furiously planning every detail. No slip-ups.

She parks down the block from Mark's address, but she's still close enough to see his front door.

She doesn't have to wait long until a dark-colored Lexus pulls up to the house and honks its horn.

Shit, it's George!

She watches Mark exit the house from the side and get into the Lexus. She knows she has to wait now, at least until he comes back.

The hours pass and the sun starts to set. It's early evening, and Mindy hasn't moved since she parked. Still, no sign of Mark.

Where the fuck did they go?

She pulls out her phone and calls George. "Hey, George."

"Hey! You get to Omaha?"

"Yeah, just now," she lies. "What are you doing?"

"Nothing, just taking Mark home." His voice turns somber. "You won't believe what happened."

"What?" she asks, but she already has an idea of what he's going to say.

"That girl Jessica, from last night...had a heart attack at the club and died."

She waits for a moment, taking the time to muster up her best 'shocked' voice. "What? You're playing..."

"No, I'm serious."

She draws out another silent moment. "What was her last name?" she asks.

"Mark says it's Larson. Jessica Larson."

"Oh my God...does her family know?" she asks. Even though she's purely acting, her sympathy is genuine.

"Yeah, early this morning."

"That's so sad," she says. She can feel her heart pumping furiously.

"Yeah," George says softly. "She was only twenty-one."

"Yeah, that's too bad...but hey, George, I'll call you here in a bit.

Tanya's calling."

"Okay, talk to you soon."

She disconnects and waits.

She watches the Lexus pull into the driveway twenty minutes later. Mindy readies herself and waits for George to leave. She pulls out a black hat and grabs a black sweater from her bag. She grabs the gun and clip from the front pocket and situates it under the sweater. She waits until George is out of sight to make any movement.

Before getting out of the car, she scans her surroundings. It's a pretty quiet neighborhood, which is going to make getting in and out easy. This needs to be as low key as possible.

She gets out and walks the short distance to Mark's. When she gets to the porch, she slows her pace. The house looks old, and she doesn't want to chance a squeaky board blowing her cover. She creeps up the few steps to his front door and listens. Through the door, she can hear Mark in a heated conversation.

"I'm working on it!... No, I don't want to go to prison! I need more time to be able to set George up!... Yes! I'll set it up--You just do your job and make sure I get credit for all this!" he yells. She hears what sounds like the phone hitting the ground. "Fucking cops want everything done now!"

She grabs the gun under her sweater and slowly counts to three. In one swift motion, she kicks in the cheap door, automatically aiming the gun at Mark's chest.

He turns, stunned. "What the...Mindy?" he asks.

She says nothing as she unloads two hollow point rounds into his chest. She watches him hit the ground and stands by his squirming body. "This is for Jessica," she says, pulling the trigger one last time. The bullet is buried in his forehead, and he goes limp.

She hurries back to her car and checks the streets again. Nothing seems urgent, so she pulls away, playing it cool. She gets back to the hotel and disassembles the gun.

I need to get rid of this.

She gets all her stuff packed up and checks out. On the way to the airport, she makes various stops around some cornfields. She throws a piece of the gun into every field she stops at. When she gets to Des Moines, she sees a dam just off the freeway. She parks on a little, gravel side road by the dam and throws the remaining pieces into the river.

At the airport, she turns in her rental and buys a plane ticket to

Chicago. She goes over every detail in her head multiple times as she makes her way to the boarding gate.

I got rid of the gun, the clothing and didn't leave anything behind. This will just be another case left unsolved.

The flight to Chicago is fast. As soon as she's off the plane, she calls Quick. "Hey, where you at?"

"I'm at home, why?" he asks.

"Come pick me up."

"Where?"

"I'm at the airport."

She can hear some shuffling on his end. "Okay, I'll be there in twenty minutes."

Within the hour, Mindy and Quick are back at the condo. They walk in, and Tanya jumps up in excitement. "Mindy!" Tanya says in a happy voice.

"Hey, Cousin!"

"You didn't call," Tanya points out.

"Yeah, I figured I had it under control," she replies.

Tanya smiles. "That's my girl! You're learning! So, what

happened?"

Images of Jessica flood her mind. "Fucking dude gave his drink to some young girl named Jessica Larson, and she took that powder you gave me."

Tanya shakes her head in disappointment. "Damn...poor girl. Well, we'll find the family and send them something to help out. You took care of Mark, right?" Tanya asks.

"Yeah...not like an accident though."

"It's okay. No witnesses and no evidence, right?"

"Yep, just like you taught me."

"Good, real good."

SMOKE JR.

Fucking Guzman's...they better give me the good shit this time. Shit last time was junk!

Smoke Jr. is in the grocery store owned by the Guzman's, but he's not there for groceries. He's headed to the back office. Two large men stand on either side of the closed office door. As he approaches, the man on the left side of the door puts a hand up.

"I'm here to see Mr. Guzman," Junior says.

The man on the right steps forward and gives him a quick pat-down. "He's clean," right man says.

Left man nods. "Okay, go ahead."

He enters the office to find Marco Guzman sitting behind his desk. His right hand man, Roberto, is sitting by the wall in a simple plastic chair.

Marco looks up when Junior opens the door. "Oh, Junior, come and sit!" Marco says in very broken English.

"How was everything, Junior?" Roberto asks.

"Before we begin," he says, pulling out his gun and placing it on the desk, "looks like you need some better help."

Marco spits in frustration. "Fucking idiots...can never find good help anymore." Marco pounds his fist on the desk. "AYE!"

The two men outside the office step in, and Marco walks around his desk to stand in front of them. He yells at the men in Spanish. Junior can pick out a few words here and there, but it's easy to understand the gist of what Marco is screaming.

The man who patted him down just moment ago steps forward. Marco grabs the gun from the desk and shoots the man in the head. The man falls to the ground, and a pool of blood expands on the floor.

Marco looks at the other man. "Now, you clean it up, or you're next!"

The nervous bodyguard nods quickly. "Yes sir, Mr. Guzman!" The man is out the door instantly.

Marco turns back around to face him. "Where were we?"

"I got a problem with that stuff you gave me," he says.

Roberto jumps in. "What kind of problem?"

"It's junk! No one wants it!"

"Junk?" Marco asks. "It's the same we've always been giving you."

"Well, no one wants it! They keep talking about how it's not as sparkly as the other stuff running around."

"'Sparkly?' What do you mean 'sparkly?'"

Junior shrugs. "You tell me. I'm just telling you what my people told me."

Marco sits in silence. After a moment, his brows furrow. "It's that damned Tanya Zaragosa; I know it! I'm going to kill that stupid bitch! She won't get away with this!"

"What do we do?" Roberto asks.

"Get Papi on the phone. We need to find out what this new stuff is," Marco says.

Roberto nods. "Yes, sir." He pulls a phone from a drawer in the office desk and begins to punch in numbers. He makes sure it rings before handing it over to Marco.

"This secure?" Marco asks.

"Yes, Sir," Roberto replies.

Marco places the phone to his ear. "Hello, Papi, how are you doing?... Yes, I'm doing good. I called because I need to know what Tanya is up to. She is killing our business. No one is wanting to buy our product, and I have a feeling she is behind all this." There is a moment of silence. "What colored boy? What's his name?... They call him what?

What the hell kind of name is that?" More silence. "Okay, Papi, keep me posted if anything else happens," he says, and then hands the phone back to Roberto.

"What did he say?" Roberto asks.

"He said Tanya has been spending a lot of time with a colored boy named Smurf, and he thinks this Smurf guy is the one doing it."

Anger builds inside of him. Smurf...the reason his family and close friends are dead. "Did you say 'Smurf?'"

Marco eyes him. "Yes...you know him?"

"I do know him... He's the same little nigga that killed my folks and got me jammed up. He's from out south."

"Well, he is stealing our clients. We need him out of the picture. With him gone, we can regain our business," Marco says.

He steps forward. "Well, Sir, if I could, I'd like to kill that little nigga's ass myself. It's personal, and I need to return the favor to his punk ass."

Marco gives a slight smile and considers. "Okay, Junior, he's all yours. Don't fuck this up... We need him out of the way. No more him, no more Tanya. I will not be run out of business by some little tramp.

Try and get some of this sparkly dope… I want to see this so-called 'sparkly' cocaine."

"Okay, Sir, I'll get on it," he replies. He knows exactly where to go.

He leaves and drives to one of his regular dope houses. He enters to see his buddy, Lazy, sprawled on the couch. He lifts his head at the sound of the door. "What's up, Family? You get me that other coke?"

"Actually, Family, that's why I'm here," he says. He sits in the recliner opposite the couch.

"You told me earlier you could get it," Lazy accuses.

"Yeah, I can, but I'd rather do business with you."

"Why?"

"I need a favor."

"What's up?"

"Call your dude and get me an ounce. I'll give you the loot for it."

"No problem," Lazy replies.

While Lazy calls his supplier, Junior gets up and heads to the kitchen for a beer. He returns just as Lazy hangs up. He sits back in the recliner and cracks open the can. "How much I owe you?"

"$1,100."

"$1,100?" he asks, shocked.

"Yeah, Family. The going rate is $200 a gram on the street."

He gives an exasperated sigh and digs in his pocket for cash. He counts out $1,100 and tosses it on the coffee table. "Okay, here's the money. I'm going to bounce. Text me when it gets here. Tell him your cousin wants to see it."

"Okay, I will," Lazy says.

He leaves and heads to the corner gas station to fill up his car with gas and get some blunt wraps. He decides to wait at the gas station, not wanting to go far. He's almost done rolling a blunt when his phone vibrates.

Dude's here family. Hurry the fuck up.

He hurries to finish the blunt and places it behind his ear. Back at Lazy's, he's faced with a young black dude he's never seen before.

"Where this shit at?" he asks, getting straight to the point. The dude pulls out a baggy and tosses it to him. He pulls out a pebble and examines it.

This shit really is sparkly...

"So you want it or not?" the dude asks.

"What's the hurry, Family?" he asks.

"Just trying to make my rounds, cuz."

"How much I owe you?"

"$1,100."

He nods to Lazy, who pulls the wad of cash from his pocket. "Count it for the man," he tells Lazy.

Lazy starts counting the bills while the dude watches. The two are so focused on the money that neither notice him reach into his waistband. Neither of them hear the click of the safety.

Junior raises his gun. "Hey, Family!"

"What's up?" the dude asks, and then he looks up. His eyes widen as he realizes he's staring down the barrel of a gun.

POW! POW!

Two bullets hit the dude's face. He's dead before he even hits the ground.

Lazy's hands fly up to his head, and his breathing stops for a split second. "Fuck, Smoke! Tell me when you're going to do shit like this! How am I going to get rid of him?"

Junior puts the gun back in his waistband. "Call the cleaners,

Family." He pulls the blunt from behind his ear and hands it to Lazy. "Here, relax. Spark it up."

Lazy accepts and lights the end, taking vigorous puffs.

"Shit, Family, pass that shit! Puff, puff, pass, Fam!" he says, breaking any lingering tension with laughter.

Lazy smiles as he passes the blunt to him. He takes a few hits and passes it back. As Lazy takes it a second time, Junior puts the cocaine into his pocket and tosses $500 in $100 bills to Lazy.

"This is for your help, Family," he says.

"Thanks, Cuz."

At the Guzman grocery store, the bodyguard who survived earlier searches him. The man does a thorough pat down this time. "I'll hold onto this," the man says as he grabs the gun off Junior. The man opens the door for him and escorts him inside.

"Good news, Junior?" Roberto asks as the door closes behind him.

He sits down and slides the cocaine across the desk. "You tell me."

Marco opens the baggie and starts examining it. He puts a little on his finger and tastes it. His face automatically looks disgusted. "It's better! How much was it?"

"$1,100," he says.

Roberto grabs some of the cocaine and starts looking at it, hardly convinced. "It really *is* sparkly."

"Fucking Tanya! What is she mixing into this?" Marco asks.

"Sir, it's Smurf mixing...not Tanya. I can almost guarantee it," he replies.

"Well, if you're right, we need him out of the way, and it needs to be done very soon. We can't afford to lose any more clientele."

"I'm on it, Sir," he replies.

Marco turns to Roberto. "Roberto, pay him the $1,100 for this." Then he turns to Junior. "This is the last time I want to hear of or even see this shit, understand?" Marco says.

He nods in agreement. Roberto pulls out a sleeve of crisp $100 bills and hands them to him.

"Thanks," he says as he puts in his pocket. He gets up, they say their farewells and he leaves.

Outside the office door, he stops by the bodyguard. "My gun," he says, holding out his hand. The bodyguard glares at him and shoves the gun into his open palm. Junior smirks and continues to his car.

Back at his place, his first thought is to devise a plan. Marco wants Smurf gone, and he's happy to fulfill the request.

I think I got that nigga, Smurf's, cell phone number around here somewhere.

He digs through drawers and piles of papers. After a while, he finally finds it. Smurf's number is scribbled on the back of a receipt. He remembers getting it from some dude right after he got out prison. *I wonder if the little nigga will answer if I call… It's probably changed already, but I'll try it.*

He dials the number, and it rings. He lets it ring six times and decides to try a different tactic. Just as he's about to end the call, a voice answers. "Hello?"

It's him. He'd recognize that voice anywhere.

"Talk," Smurf says after a few seconds of silence.

"What's up, Family?" he says.

"Who's this?" Smurf asks.

"A ghost," he replies.

The other end of the line goes silent for a moment. "I recognize this voice…yeah, this sounds like that bitch-ass nigga, Smoke Jr."

"Bitch-ass nigga, huh?" he replies in anger.

"Yep."

His blood boils. "You will be seeing a nigga, Family soon! REAL FUCKIN' SOON!"

"Well, when I see you, be sure to tell that bitch-ass father of yours I said 'hi.'"

He speaks through gritted teeth. "You can tell him yourself, Nigga. You'll be seeing him before I do."

Smurf laughs on the other end. "Just like your dad...thinking you're all bad."

"Better watch your back, Smurf, because the day you slip is the day I'll be there."

Smurf laughs again. "Oh, scary!" he says in a mocking tone.

"Just wait, you can tell that nigga, Jeff, 'hey' for me."

This comment gets to Smurf, and his laughter turns to anger. "Fuck you, Nigga! I'll be seeing you soon...that's if you got the balls!" The line goes dead as Smurf ends the call.

He's satisfied that he at least got to Smurf, but the anger is still fresh in him.

Fuck that nigga, Smurf! He's a dead man walking! He's gonna slip up, and I'll be there to add one more hole to that big-ass head of his.

He tosses the phone on the table and sits back on his couch. Thoughts flood his consciousness. Among the waves, it hits him.

They say Tanya is nothing without him, so he's nothing without her. I'll kill two birds with one stone. Catch her slipping and get her ass, Fuck chasing him. Shit, best way to get him is to get them to come to me, and she's exactly how I'll do just that. I'll be seeing you soon, Smurf, very soon.

QUICK

"What up, Sis?" he answers. Mindy's on the other end of the line.

"Alex, I dropped off George's car at the Lexus dealership to get some work done on it and they won't give me a loaner because it's not mine... Can you give me a ride back to the condo?" she asks.

"Man, Sis, I'm really busy. I'm in the middle of something right now."

"I don't care what you're doing! You're coming to pick me up, Alex!" she yells.

He laughs, amused by her girlish temper. "Okay, okay, okay! I'll come get you in twenty minutes, but you have to drive me around 'til I'm done. Then I will drop you off, cool?"

"Okay, I'll do your bitch work. You better be happy you're my brother, because if you weren't..."

He laughs again. "Don't tell me! I'll be there soon, alright?"

"Okay," she replies and hangs up.

He arrives at the dealership to find Mindy looking at the new Lexus LS 400 Sedan. He honks his horn twice to get her attention. At the sound of the car horn, she walks to his car, and he gets out, letting her into the driver's seat.

"What are we doing?" she asks, closing the car door.

"Errands," he replies after his door closes.

"Are they dirty?"

He shakes his head. "No, just debt collecting.

They leave the dealership, and he directs her to the first stop. "Pull

over here and wait for me... I won't be but just a few minutes." Mindy

shifts in her seat, annoyed, and puts the car in park.

He gets out and walks down the sidewalk towards the house. As he

approaches, he sees a black Range Rover.

That looks like that nigga, Smoke's, truck...

He moves cautiously to the front yard. When he gets to the front

walkway, he stops. The front door creaks open, and within seconds, he's

staring into the eyes of Smoke Jr.

Fucking, bitch-ass nigga!

Two goons emerge from the open door. He notices Jr. reaching for

his gun, but he's quick on the draw. He pulls out his gun with

remarkable speed and unloads shot after shot.

As the three men run for cover, he hides behind a nearby parked car. The men return fire, and the peaceful silence of the neighborhood vanishes. This house and the street have quickly become a war zone as gunshots ring through the crisp, warm air.

He turns and looks for Mindy. She's already out of the car and along its backside, gun in hand.

If I distract them, she can take them all out.

He reaches around the back bumper, firing wild shots. Most of them end up hitting the house. He pulls back and hears their gunfire and then a yell.

"I'm hit!" an unfamiliar male voice shouts.

He peeks out from his location and sees one of the goons lying on the ground. He fires two shots.

One hits the man in the chest, and the other tears through his face. He watches the man go instantly limp.

Without pause, the man to Junior's left drops as the back of his head explodes and brain splatters against the side of the house. He fires another shot, hitting Junior in the leg. The shot only wounds him, and Junior. scrambles back into the house.

Mindy hops into the car and speeds up to get him. She slams on the brakes when she gets to him and floors it before he's even fully inside the car.

"THE FUCK WAS THAT?" she yells.

"That fucking nigga, Smoke Jr...the one who shot me!"

"Are you okay, Alex?"

He nods. "I'm good. Are you okay?"

"Yeah, them fools can't shoot for shit."

"Thanks for the help, Sis. I was stuck behind that car."

"No one fucks with my family, that's for sure! We need to tell Tanya," she says.

"Where is she?"

She's at the restaurant, which is exactly where we're going."

At the restaurant, Mindy is stopped by one of the security guards standing outside the office door.

"Out of my way!" she yells as she pushes the man aside. She opens the door, and Quick follows behind her. Tanya is sitting in a chair across the room, engrossed in her phone. "Tanya!" Mindy yells.

Tanya's head snaps up. "Mindy! Are you okay?"

Quick steps forward. "Cousin, we have a problem."

Tanya's brow furrows. "What is it?"

"Well, I had Mindy take me to one of my spots to pick up some money. I noticed a Range Rover at the first spot we dropped by. It looked like Smoke Jr.'s, but I know for a fact he doesn't mess with that dude. So, I don't know why he was there."

Concern spreads across Tanya's face. "What happened?"

"Well, I got to the front yard, and he and two of his goons came out. Then all hell broke out! Bullets flying everywhere... We killed the two goons he was with, and I hit that nigga, Smoke, in his leg."

"You guys didn't get hit, right? I mean, you guys are okay?"

"Yes, we're fine," he assures her.

"Okay, you two just relax. Now, what would make Jr. come snooping around our territory?... Has anything strange happened lately?" Tanya asks.

"Well, I *did* give some shit to Lil' B a few days ago, and now he's nowhere to be found. It's not like him to pull some shady shit."

"Do you know who he was going to see?"

He shakes his head. "No, but I can find out."

"Well, when you do, you and Smurf pay him a visit and get any information by any means necessary."

"Okay," he replies.

Tanya continues. "This shit is going to end. I have a feeling they are going to attempt a takeover, and the only people crazy enough to try it are Smoke's suppliers--the Guzman's. If they have the nerve to attack us on *our* territory, we're going to kill them on theirs. No one, I mean NO ONE, messes with our family and lives to tell about it. Especially Marco... He's been alive for too long. After all that he's done to our family, I don't care who dies in their family...women, children, OR men. If you can get a clean kill, then do it. They want to see a ruthless bitch; I'll give them one. I want the Guzman family name gone from this planet. You two understand?"

Mindy and Quick nod in agreement.

"Okay, Mindy, come with me. Quick, meet with Smurf and figure out who your buddy went to go see. And if you and Smurf catch Smoke, get rid of him."

He nods and leaves.

When he gets to Smurf's house, he pulls in the drive way and honks twice. In the car, he explains the situation and their current task. They make a few stops. Smurf drives and waits in the car while Quick collects debts and asks questions.

At the last stop, he gets back in the car and smiles. "Well, Smurf, I found out who Lil' B was going to see."

"Who?" Smurf asks.

"Some dude named Lazy."

Smurf stares at him. "Lazy is one of Smoke's little homies."

"Oh, you know him?" he asks.

"No, I just know of him. He's a real shady nigga, that's for sure. You know where he's staying at?" Smurf asks.

"Yeah, dude told me. You want to pay him a visit?"

"Yeah," Smurf says, putting the car into gear. "Let's drop off this cash first, then go."

They pull up a block away from Lazy's address. Smurf puts the car in park and turns to Quick. "Okay, Bro, be cool. You get him to open the door, and then we'll rush him. Remember what your cousin said: *Any means necessary.*

He nods, and they get out. It's a short walk, but within minutes they're at the front door. He knocks and a voice from inside the house yells, "Who is it?"

"It's Quick; open up."

"Who?" the voice yells back.

"It's Quick, Nigga! Open up!"

Multiple locks start clicking. "Who is it?" the voice asks one more time as the door begins to creep open.

BANG!

Smurf kicks the door open as soon as the knob starts to turn. The sudden jolt knocks Lazy to the ground. As he hits the ground, the gun in his hand falls onto the floor. Lazy tries to scramble for it, but Smurf already has his gun pulled out and against the back of Lazy's head.

"Stop, before I splatter your brains all over your floor," Smurf says in his deep voice.

Lazy goes still. Quick closes and locks the door while Smurf drags Lazy into the kitchen. He forces Lazy to get up and shoves him into a chair. "Sit the fuck down!" Smurf yells.

"What do you want?" Lazy finally manages to speak.

"Where's Lil' B at!"

"I don't know! He stopped by a while ago; haven't seen him since!"

Smurf stares at him, then hits him in the face with the butt of his gun. "Where is Lil' B!" he yells again.

Lazy rears back from the blow. "Fuck you both!"

Smurf beats him with the gun again, this time knocking him to the ground. Quick steps in and kneels next to Lazy. "Now, Lazy, my friend here...he doesn't like you. Honestly, he really wants to kill you. But if you can help us, we might spare your life." Lazy coughs in pain. "So can you help us?" he asks.

Lazy raises his head and looks at Smurf's gun, then back at Quick. After a minute, he speaks. "It was Smoke."

Quick smiles. "There we go. Look how easy that was. Now, what about Smoke?"

"Smoke wanted the Coke I'd been getting, so I called Lil' B to get it. I didn't know he was going to shoot him."

"So Smoke killed Lil' B?" Quick asks. Lazy just stares at him. "What do you know about Smoke? Do have an address on him?"

Lazy stays quiet.

"Oh, it's like that?" Smurf says. He lets off a bullet into Lazy's left knee.

Lazy screams in pain. "Son of a bitch!"

"Now answer the question before your right one gets it, too," Smurf says, aiming his gun at the other knee.

Lazy puts his hand up, still grunting and breathing heavy from the pain. "All I know is that he goes to some grocery store to talk to his bosses. I don't have a name or anything, I just know he took the ounce and went back to show them. That's all I know; I swear!"

Quick looks from Lazy to Smurf. "I bet they're trying to figure out what's in it. I know it," he says.

Smurf looks at Lazy again. "Is that it? That's worthless information!" He clicks the hammer back in the gun.

"Wait, wait! I swear I don't know anything else!"

Smurf starts to count. "One…"

"Wait! I remember something… I remember Smoke saying something about meeting his bosses soon, like in the next few days at the grocery store!"

"Thanks," Smurf says. He aims his gun higher and puts a bullet in the temple area of Lazy's skull.

Back in the car, they go over the new information.

"So, all we know is that the Guzman family is desperate. They are trying to figure out the cut we use, and they're going to be meeting at the grocery store soon…" he says, trailing off.

"Worthless information," Smurf replies.

"No, it could be good. We might be able to catch them all at once and wipe out the main part of the family."

Smurf shakes his head. "I don't think they are dumb enough to let people know their business," Smurf says.

"You know how it is, Smurf. Niggas talk a lot."

"True story...so what next?" Smurf asks.

"We tell Tanya. She'll know what to do."

They go back to the restaurant and head to the office again. Tanya's waiting for them when they open the door. "So... what did you guys find out?" she asks.

"Well, pretty much, they are trying to figure out the cut we are using that's making our shit sell so fast. We also found out there's going to be a family meeting at their grocery store in the next few days," Quick relays.

"Okay, you two stake out the grocery store, and let me know what and who you see. Anything strange, you call me."

He nods. The war has begun.

Over the next few days, Smurf and Quick keep a close eye on the

Guzman grocery store. It's not until almost a week goes by that they start to see anything new. It's well after closing hours for the grocery store, but there seems to be a lot of traffic going in. Nothing comes out.

"It must be happening," he says to Smurf.

"Yeah, but Tanya said to just keep tabs."

A car pulls up, and a dark, skinny man gets out. As the man gets closer, Quick recognizes him.

"What the fuck... That's my uncle, Papi! What is he doing here?"

"Are you sure?" Smurf asks.

"Yes, I know it's my uncle! That was him!"

Smurf pulls out his phone and calls Tanya. After she answers, he passes it to Quick.

"Hello?"

"Hey, where's Papi?" he asks.

"Out of town, why?"

"Because I just watched him walk into the grocery store."

It's quiet on Tanya's end. "It's not him, it can't be...maybe just someone who resembles him. But, hey, I'm gonna call you back... Give me one second," she replies, then hangs up.

The phone rings a few minutes later. "Hey, I talked to him, and he said he is still out of town."

"Okay, it might have been my eyes playing games. I'll let you know what else happens." He ends the call.

Almost two hours pass before people finally start to come out of the store.

"Hey, there's that dude," he says to Smurf. "Tanya said it's not him, but I have a feeling she's wrong."

They watch him get into his car and drive off. They follow at a safe distance for half an hour and watch as the car pulls into a parking garage. The parking garage of Papi's building.

He looks at Smurf. "Now do you believe me? This is our uncle's parking lot."

"What was he doing with the Guzman's, and why is he lying to Tanya?" Smurf asks.

Anger runs through Quick. "I don't know, but if he's up to something, we are going to catch him slipping."

PAPI

"Papi?... Papi, are you paying attention?" Tanya says from her side of the desk.

"Yes, I'm paying attention," he replies.

"Okay, good, you looked like you were spacing out."

He shakes his head. "I'm fine. Continue," he responds.

"I need you to get ahold of the soldiers and set up a hit."

He raises a brow. "On?"

"The Guzman family grocery store. I want it burned to the ground," she says with venom.

"When?"

"As soon as possible."

He nods. "Yes ma'am, I'll make the call today."

"Okay, good," she says with a smirk. "Since that is taken care of, how was your trip?"

"My trip?" he asks, but catches himself. "Oh! It was good."

"Where did you go?"

"St. Louis," he responds.

"For?"

He gives her a skeptical look. "Cardinals game... What's up with the interrogation?"

She shrugs. "No reason. I was just curious, that's all."

He's still a bit skeptical, but just nods slowly. "Well, you need anything else? So I can go get started with this, I mean."

"No, I'm good," she replies.

He leaves and gets in his car, mulling over his current task.

Fuck...how am I going to do this? I can't let the Guzman's get run out by my niece...but if I tip them off, they'll find out I told them... I need to talk to Marco.

He pulls out his throwaway phone and calls Marco.

"Hello, Papi," Marco answers.

"Hey, we need to talk...in person."

"Where and when?"

"Holiday Inn, downtown in an hour," he says.

"Okay, I'll be there. See you soon."

Papi's at the hotel twenty minutes before their scheduled meeting time. He picks up a copy of the newspaper and finds a chair in the lobby. Within ten minutes, Marco walks through the front entrance. They exchange their usual greetings, and he leads them to the empty hotel bar. They choose a table in the farthest corner and sit.

"I called you down here because I want to know how much longer."

"'Til what?" Marco asks.

"'Til you can finally be Don Marco again."

"Yes, well...that's what I wanted to ask you, Papi... You need to give Tanya up. She and that nigga of hers have been causing a lot of problems for this takeover. It looks like the only way this will work is with them completely out of the picture."

He sits back in his chair and looks at Marco, but stays quiet.

"Hey, Papi, don't be getting all soft on me now. You were okay picking off your brother and his son... So what's a few more?"

He glares at him. "You're asking me to kill off my family, Marco."

"Well, sometimes you have to give up a lot to gain even more."

He places his hand on his head and rubs his fingers through his hair. It takes a long moment before he can speak. "What do you want from me, Marco?"

"I just need a set up...an hour window, tops, where Tanya and this Smurf character will be alone, with no bodyguards. I will do the rest."

"If I do this, it's over. I got my own family to worry about."

"With those two gone, the Zaragosa family business will be all yours."

His glare hardens. "Okay, fine. I will do it."

"That's what I want to hear, Papi," Marco says, smiling.

"Just stay away from the store for a while. I'll buy you two days to get Tanya and that little nigga boyfriend of hers. But just so you know...she put a hit on your whole family *and* your store."

Marco raises his eyebrows in mock surprise. "Is that right? Then, she'll be surprised to see my face before she dies. She's going to remember my face forever."

"Today, Marco, is the day I have to put the hit out...so get it done soon," he says.

"Just get them alone, and I will take care of them," Marco responds.

"I'll call you soon with a location and time."

"Okay, Papi, just keep me updated. I'll have my people waiting."

"I will, Marco," he replies as he gets up from the table. "I will call you later." He shakes Marco's hand and leaves the bar.

Back in his car, he thinks about the decision he just made and how he is going to complete the task at hand.

How can I get her and Smurf together without drawing attention?

He thinks over the next few hours, coming up with different places, different scenarios. Each idea has its obvious flaws, but then he finds one that's sure to work.

I'll get them to meet me at the docks. I'll say we have a problem with a shipment. Not much traffic and not many witnesses.

He pulls out his phone and calls Tanya.

"Hello?"

"Hey, niece."

"What's going on, uncle?"

"We got a problem."

"What kind of problem?" she asks.

"Can you and Smurf meet me at the docks tonight? It has to do with our shipment."

"Yes, we will be there. What time?"

"Meet me there at 11:00."

"Okay, uncle, we'll see you at 11:00," she responds.

He hangs up and tosses his phone into the passenger seat.

Bliss 2

This better fucking work, Marco. This better fucking work.

MARCO

Roberto sits with Marco in the tiny office again. There's a lot going on at the moment, but for the time being, he lets his mind wander to distant memories.

"Roberto, it's been a long time...a very long, time that we've had to share our beloved city with the disgrace of the Zaragosas. I still remember it like yesterday, when we first started the family here in Chicago."

Roberto looks up from the magazine he's reading and nods. "Me too, Marco. Me too."

He smiles. "It's been a long time, my friend."

"Yes it has, Marco. But it's almost here."

He nods. "Yes, yes it is. Do you remember the first time we started doing business with Junior's father?"

"Smoke? I do... We were new to the city, and he helped us to become the second largest cocaine family in Chicago...behind those greedy Zaragosas," Roberto says.

"Yeah, he was a good man. It's too bad he is gone."

"Yes, he was a dear friend to us. Very loyal and trustworthy."

"You're right, Roberto," he says. "That's why I promised him that no matter what happens, I will always treat Junior like one of my own. I've done what I promised."

"Junior...he's been molded to be a great asset to this family, as well."

He agrees again. "Yeah, he has. I can't wait to finally get him his own family when this is over. That idiot, Papi, is just like his brother, Albert...so greedy...so money hungry that it blinds his judgment."

"That's what makes him a great pawn in this big game, Marco. He's easily influenced by the promise of money and power."

"It's great, isn't it? The idiot sold out his own blood for money. If he only knew he was just a puppet in all of this," he says with childlike glee.

"He's worthless to us... If he would sell out his own blood, he would definitely sell us out to the highest bidder. It will be great to watch their faces right before we kill them. All three of them," Roberto says.

"You're right, Roberto. Ever since my son was killed by that little bitch Tanya at the strip club, I've had a personal vendetta against that whole family. I want to make her suffer as much as she has made me suffer. It will be a satisfying image to watch that bitch take her last breath...knowing my face is the last one she sees. And she'll remember me forever. Once Papi does as he is told and brings us Tanya and Smurf, this city will be ours for the taking, and no one will stop us. We will finally be the biggest cocaine family in the Windy City."

Roberto stands and raises an invisible glass in front of him. "To the long-awaited downfall of the Zaragosa family, to the new expansion of the Guzman family and to Papi...the greedy bastard. If it wasn't for him, this never would have happened," Roberto says.

Marco smiles at Roberto and raises his own imaginary glass. "To Papi and the Zaragosa's: May they all burn in hell." He revels in the moment, then shifts back to reality. "Roberto, get the men ready to move at any time."

"Yes, Sir. I'm on it," Roberto says, taking a slight bow before leaving the office.

Now we wait.

QUICK

"I can't believe that motherfucker! My own fucking blood!" he yells, knocking a kitchen chair across the floor.

"He was meeting with Marco?" Smurf asks.

"Man! I followed him into the hotel! And what do I find? Them having a meeting in the hotel bar!"

"Did you hear what was being said?"

"No! I couldn't get close enough... They were in the back of the bar."

Smurf pulls out his phone and hands it to him. "Call Tanya."

He's so flustered, he doesn't even know where to begin, but he takes the phone and dials the number.

"Hey, Honey," she answers.

"Hey, Tanya, it's Quick. I'm calling on Smurf's phone."

"Oh, well what's up?"

"We caught Papi's ass again!"

"What?" she says.

"I've been following his car for the past few hours, and he ended up at the Holiday Inn downtown."

"So what?"

"Well, no big deal...'til fucking Marco showed up! So, I snuck into the hotel in case he was trying to sneak on uncle...and I find them having a meeting in the back of the hotel bar!"

"Could you hear their discussion?" she asks.

"No!" he says in angry dismay. "I couldn't get close enough..."

"Where is he at now?"

"We are following him—we're downtown. Man, cousin, I wanted to smoke them both right there in the hotel bar...but I just couldn't do it! I just couldn't hurt Papi...he's family."

She stops him. "Enough talk like that. Just follow him, and when he goes back home, you call me. We'll pay him a visit and see what he has to say about this." She ends the call.

They do as they're told and follow him, always making sure to keep a safe distance. After a while, Smurf gets agitated. "Fuck! This dude is stopping at every place in the city he possibly can!"

He turns to look at Smurf. "You think he knows we're following him?"

"No," Smurf responds. "Papi thinks too hard. He misses the easy stuff. We've been out in the open enough, plus we're in a rental, so he doesn't know what to look for."

"Well, I hope he gets tired of driving around, because I'm sick of this shit, that's for sure."

After another twenty minutes and two stops, they watch him pull into his parking garage.

"Finally!" he says in a thankful voice. "Hey, call Tanya and tell her we are here."

"Alright," Smurf responds as he picks up his phone.

Quick continues watching Papi, monitoring every move. He hardly notices the phone conversation, but after a few minutes he's jarred back to reality. Smurf nudges his arm. "She said she will be down here soon--just stay put and if he leaves, we call her."

He turns back to look at the parking garage again. This time, he's thankful for Papi taking his time. He can't risk losing him now.

Another few minutes pass and Smurf's phone rings. Smurf answers, but says little. The call is short, and he takes the phone from his ear.

Quick looks at him anxiously. "What did she say, Smurf?"

"She said that she told him we were in the neighborhood and were going to stop by... I wonder what Tanya is going to do to him."

Anger flares inside Quick again. "I hope she kills his traitorous ass for fucking over his own family--his own blood in favor for them fucking Guzman's! I hope he rots in hell with the whole Guzman family."

TANYA

She pulls into the parking garage of Papi's condo and pulls out her phone.

"Hello?" the manly voice says.

"Hello, uncle, what are you doing?"

"I'm at home... What's going on?"

"Nothing," she says. "I'm actually going to stop by real quick."

"Why?" he asks. "I'm kind of busy right now."

"It will just be for a minute. I have to meet Quick and Smurf soon."

He hesitates before answering her. "Okay, come on over." She hangs up and gets out of her car.

Papi has been acting kind of shady lately...all of the lies, pressing to get things done... I hope he has a good reason for his actions. I would hate having to kill my own uncle...

She gets to his door and knocks.

"Come in!" Papi yells from the other side.

She goes inside and finds Papi at the kitchen table eating dinner. "Hello, uncle."

He just nods and continues to eat. She pulls her phone from her purse and sends Quick a text.

Call me.

He finishes his bite before speaking. "So, what's going on Tanya?" he asks.

"Nothing too much, uncle...just stopping by to see what's up and talk to Quick and Smurf." She pauses briefly. "What did you want to tell me at the docks tonight?"

Her phone chimes loudly with a call.

Just in time.

"Hold that thought, uncle," she says before answering. "Hello?"

"Okay, we're coming," Quick says on the other end.

"Okay, I'm at uncle's."

"We'll be there soon."

"Okay, see you soon," she says, then ends the call.

Papi finishes another bite before asking, "Who was that, Tanya?"

"That was Quick. He is going to stop by for a minute—he's in the neighborhood. He needed to talk to me about something." She watches him eat and waits until he's almost done chewing. "Oh, so what's up with that stuff you wanted to tell me?"

Papi swallows. "Well we have a problem... Some shipments are late."

"Late? What do you mean, late?"

"I'm still trying to figure it out," Papi says.

"Hello?" a loud voice calls from the hallway.

They both turn towards the door. "Yeah!" Tanya yells. "We're in the kitchen!"

Quick and Smurf come to the entryway of the kitchen. "Hello, Family," Quick says, but continues down the hall to the bathroom.

Smurf stops beside Tanya. "What's up?" he says as he gives her a kiss.

From the corner of her eye, she notices the glare on her uncle's face when Smurf kisses her. Inwardly, she smiles.

They continue with idle chitchat, catching up and laughing. Papi is caught up in the family moment, making him oblivious to anything else going on around him. Smurf has started to move around to the other side of the table, avoiding doing anything suspicious. Papi's back is to him.

Tanya watches as Smurf pulls his gun from his waistband, cocks the hammer and places it at the nape of Papi's neck.

"Stay still, Papi," Smurf says in a low, soft voice.

"What do you think you're going to do with that?" Papi asks.

"Blow your brains out of that thick head of yours if you answer any of these questions wrong," Smurf says.

"What questions?" He looks at Tanya.

She pulls her gun out and places it on the table. She cocks the hammer for added effect. "My questions, uncle."

He glares at her, betrayal flashing in his eyes. "Fine! Ask away!" he yells.

She doesn't hesitate. "Why have you been lying lately?"

"What have I lied about?" he says quickly in response.

"Going out of town."

"I was out of town!" Papi says in defense.

Smurf jams the gun into Papi's neck.

"You were at the Guzman family grocery store," she continues.

"No, I wasn't!"

Now, Quick jumps in. "Uncle, I've been following you around, and you've met the Guzmans twice. Once at the store and the second time at the Holiday Inn. You and Marco were sitting in the hotel bar alone!"

"Is this true, Uncle? Secret meetings with Marco?" she asks. He stares at her, but says nothing.

"Answer me, dammit!" she yells.

"Well, it looks like you already have the answer, seeing as you have your guns drawn on me."

She shakes her head in disappointment. "Why, Uncle? Why, Marco? He killed Daddy, your own brother! And your nephew!"

"They killed themselves!" he spits out. They didn't listen to me. That's all they had to do, and we could have kept the peace!"

She stares at him, disbelief and betrayal flooding over her. "Are you hearing yourself, Uncle? Please don't tell me you had something to do with Daddy and Mario's death."

Papi stays silent again.

Anger overtakes her. "Fuck, Uncle! Your own blood?! For what? Them?! Fucking Mexicans offer you a better life?! You are some piece of shit!" she yells. "I'm sick of this family! I should be the Don, not you! You gave up your own blood for money!" She takes a few quick breaths, then says through gritted teeth, "I hope you rot in hell, Uncle."

She looks at Smurf, and he lowers his gun slightly, then pulls the trigger twice, putting two shots into Papi's back. His body falls forward onto the table. She pushes him back in his chair as she watches him struggle to breathe.

She picks up her gun and points it at his head. "I loved you, Uncle...like my own father. Now, I find out you sold out your family for greed." He looks at her, shock and fear envelop his face. She closes her eyes, and a tear rolls down her cheek. She fires a single shot between his eyes, killing him instantly. She opens her eyes as another tear slowly rolls down her other cheek. "Goodbye, Uncle."

She turns to Quick. "Call the clean-up crew to take care of this." Quick nods.

Riiiiiing.

All three stop and look at each other. Another ring sounds as they look at Papi's lifeless body. Smurf starts searching Papi's pockets and pulls out a cell phone.

"This ain't one of ours," he says, scanning the phone. His expression changes when he sees the main screen.

The phone continues ringing. "Who is it?" she asks.

Smurf looks up at her. "It's Marco."

She turns to Quick "Quick, take that--you sound like uncle. Answer it, and see what he says."

Smurf tosses the phone to Quick, and he answers. "Hello, Marco."

"Hello, Papi. Did you get that set up yet?" Marco asks.

"I'm still working on it."

"Well, you need to hurry up. I got a two-day window, to take care of that bitch niece of yours and her black boyfriend, before you put in the order."

Quick is stunned at this, but keeps up the act. "Okay, I'll keep pressing on, then. I'll call you back."

"Okay, Papi. Hopefully soon."

"It will be, Marco. It will be." Quick ends the call.

"What did he say?" she asks.

"Sounds like Papi was setting you and Smurf up to get killed...something about a two-day window for Papi to put in an order," Quick says.

"Order? What order? What is he talking about?" she asks.

"Maybe a hit," Smurf says.

"I almost forgot. I put a hit out on the Guzman's grocery store that was supposed to be done today... Fucking Uncle was trying to get us killed tonight!"

"What?" Smurf replies.

"Well, he called earlier and asked you and I to meet him at the docks about a problem with our shipments... He must not have had time to call Marco and tell him."

"We should set up a meeting with Marco and smoke his ass, and then work our way down the food chain."

"How are we going to do that?" Quick asks.

"Well, you said Marco meets Papi alone...so you set up a meeting between Papi and Marco, and when he shows up, we ambush him. It will work, especially if Marco doesn't suspect anything now," Smurf replies.

Tanya takes a moment to think. "Alright, this is how we're going to do it. Quick, call Marco in the morning. Set up a time for him to meet you at the docks, tomorrow night at our boat. We will be waiting there for him to show. When he does, we have to make sure that EVERYONE with him gets on that boat. We secure it before we take off. We drive out far enough, then we'll send his ass to the fishes."

"Where did you get that idea?" Quick asks.

She shrugs. "From an old mob movie." Quick laughs.

"Shut up, Quick--just do what I tell you to do."

"Okay, okay!" he says through chuckles. "I will call Marco tomorrow in the morning, just like you said."

"Thank you," she responds. She looks at the gun in her hand.

Finally, I will be able to avenge my family's death and send that piece of shit Marco to meet his son. Soon, very soon.

JJ

"You alright?" Tanya asks. After stopping by the warehouse to check on production and found him sitting at his desk, zoned out.

JJ automatically snaps back to reality. "Yeah, I'm good Tanya. Just a little burnt out with all this work. You guys are keeping George and I very busy," he responds, yawning.

"Well, good news then! I'm taking you on a much-needed-vacation for the weekend! Have you ever been to Mexico?" she asks.

He shakes his head. "Nope, I've stayed in the states my whole life. Why?"

"Well, I have some friends down in Los Cabos. It's a nice spot to just get away and relax... If you want, I can make a call, and you can head down there for a few days," Tanya says.

He thinks it over, briefly, before responding. "Yeah, that sounds good! I need to take a few days off."

That same day, he joins Tanya and a few others for a barbecue on a pontoon. With a beer in one hand, he sits and watches other people on boats and jet skis.

I want to have my own boat someday...

He takes a drink from his beer and watches as Tanya approaches and sits down next to him. "I got ahold of my friend Sissy down there in Los Cabos."

"What did she have to say?" he asks.

"She said her weekend is free, so if you go down, she'll take you around and show you a good time."

He takes another swig. "Do I need to find a hotel?"

"No, Sissy has a house down there. You can crash at her place."

He nods. "Sounds good to me! Looks like I'll be heading to Mexico!" He stops, realizing there may be a small issue. "I need a passport, don't I?"

Tanya puts her hand up to stop him. "Don't worry about that; I'll take care of it and the flight. Just be ready to leave tonight."

He raises his brows in slight shock. "Tonight?... Okay, I can do that!"

Around 7:00PM that evening, his phone rings. He sets a duffel bag next to his suitcase and answers.

"Hey, are you ready?" It's Tanya.

"Yeah, I'm ready!"

"Okay, be outside in five minutes, and I'll pick you up out front."

"Okay, I'll see you soon," he says, then hangs up. He does a quick mental check to make sure he has everything. He grabs his wallet and his phone, but heads back to his room. He goes into his closet safe and removes $5,000 in large bills. He folds the stack in half and wraps a rubber band around it.

Back in the living room, he puts the folded stack in his duffel bag. He's learned from experience to never put anything super-valuable in checked baggage. There's no telling when or how airport security will lose it.

He grabs up his luggage and heads out the door. Outside his apartment building, he doesn't wait long. Tanya pulls up in Smurf's Cadillac truck. He throws his bags in the back seat and hops in the front. "Hey, here's your passport," she says, handing it to him.

He takes it from her hand and opens it up. "What the hell?" he says. "This isn't my name."

"Yeah, about that," she starts. "We don't use real names to travel, especially being in this type of business. We don't need any paper trails."

"Is this thing legit? I mean, I'm not going to get busted for this, right?"

"Don't worry about it; we do this all the time. Are you bringing some money with you?"

"Yeah, five grand."

She nods. "Good, that should be enough...more than enough. Before I forget, Sissy is going to pick you up at the airport. Give her a hug--tell her I miss her and send my love."

"Okay," he replies.

She pulls up to the loading terminal of the airport and parks the car. "Well, we're here! Have fun."

"Thanks Tanya, for everything."

"No big deal. If you need anything, just call. Sissy will take care of you."

He gets out, grabs his luggage, and continues through check-in.

At the terminal a private Lear jet is waiting. On board, he's greeted by a young girl in her early twenties. She reminds him of a younger version of Shakira.

"Hello, my is Melissa. I will be your stewardess for the flight, so if you need anything, just let me know. Make yourself comfortable and we'll be departing in a few minutes."

"Okay, thank you," he replies. He finds a seat near the middle of the plane and shoves his duffel bag in the overhead compartment. The seats are big and plush. He sits and leans the chair back, finding it even more comfortable than his recliner at home.

I haven't even left yet, and it already feels like the best vacation. Watch out, Los Cabos.

He closes his eyes and is asleep before the plane moves.

"Sir?...excuse me, Sir?"

He's jolted awake. "Huh? What?" he says, still half asleep.

"We are here, Sir," Melissa says gently.

"How long have I been sleeping?"

"A few hours," she says.

He leans up in his chair and looks out the window to see a plane taxiing on the runway. "Los Cabos?"

"Yes, Sir."

He stretches and waits while she opens the overhead compartment, then follows her to the jet's exit. She opens it, and he's instantly washed in early morning sunlight.

A few yards away, near the plane, is a parked Mercedes SL 500 AMG convertible. Standing next to it is a young woman who resembles Eva Mendes. She sees him and smiles. "And you must be JJ."

He returns the smile. "You must be Sissy."

She laughs. "You definitely know Tanya."

Damn, this girl is sexy! I could definitely get used to her...

"Tanya sends her love and says she misses you. And wanted me to give you a hug," he says.

He gives her a quick hug and retrieves his other bag from the jet's storage area. He throws his luggage in the trunk. "Nice wheels," he says as he gets in and closes the door.

"You like it?" she asks, a coy smile playing on her lips.

"Yes, I used to have one just like this! So where to?" he asks.

"My place, first. We'll drop off your stuff and get you settled in, then we'll figure things out from there."

"Sounds good," he says. He likes the thought of having no set plans. For now, he'll simply ride the wind.

As they pull up into her driveway, he's amazed by the size of her house. "Wow, nice place! You live here alone?"

"Yeah, for now," she says, pulling the car around to the front door.

"Is this a ranch-style home?" he asks.

"Yes, it's Mediterranean-style: Four bedrooms, four-and-a-half bathrooms. All on one level."

"Yeah, this is really nice! I just have a condo back home."

"Yeah, you can get some nice houses real cheap down here," she responds.

As they enter the home, he starts looking around.

Damn, this place looks expensive!

She gives him a tour around the home and shows him where he'll be sleeping. "I'm going to take a shower real quick," he says.

"Take your time," she replies, and then leaves.

He tosses his bag onto the bed and grabs his shower stuff. After he's clean and dressed, he gets ready and meets her in the kitchen.

She looks up from her magazine when he walks in. "So what do you want to do?" she asks.

"Let's go grab a bite to eat, and you can show me around."

She smiles. "Sounds good. I know a place you might like."

She drives him to a seafood restaurant on the outskirts of the city.

It's a beautiful place with windows all around. He follows Sissy across the restaurant to a booth in the corner. The view from their table overlooks the ocean, almost as if they're suspended over the blue giant.

They sit and, almost immediately, a waiter appears and places two large margaritas on the table.

JJ slides a glass in front of Sissy and pulls the other in front of himself.

"So, Sissy, how long have you known Tanya?"

She takes a long sip before answering. "A very long time. Her father and mine were best friends as kids growing up. She's pretty much family. How long have you known her?" she asks.

He laughs. "Nowhere near as long as you have. My friend started dating her cousin Mindy--that's how I'm met her."

"Ahh, I see," she replies.

They spend the next hour eating shrimp, conversing and drinking tequila. He leaves the restaurant feeling warm and comfortable. He slides into the passenger seat of Sissy's car, relaxed.

"So, what do you want to do now?" she asks.

"I don't care; I just want to have a good time," he responds. "So, I'm up for whatever."

She smiles. "Alright, give me one second." She pulls out her phone. She waits briefly, and then begins speaking Spanish to the individual on the other end.

Damn...she's sexy, wealthy and bilingual... Hopefully she's single... That would make the weekend so much better...

The call doesn't last long. She hangs up in a manner of seconds and turns to him. "Have you ever been on a yacht?"

He raises his eyebrows in surprise. "When you say yacht, you mean a speed boat?"

She laughs. "No, I mean over-a-hundred-foot yacht."

"Shit, no! I've seen pictures of them."

She laughs again. "Well, today is your lucky day. My friend Carlos is having a little get together on his yacht. He said we were welcome to come."

"Do I need to change? I mean, I'm just in a T-shirt and shorts."

"No, it's just a casual thing."

"Do they speak English? Because I don't speak Spanish," he responds.

She laughs. "Stop worrying about this! It's supposed to be a fun weekend! Just kick back and relax," she says, as she pats him just above the knee a few times. She starts up the car and puts the transmission into drive.

The time feels like forever as he watches the scenery pass by. He admires the large houses and their vast landscapes.

Man, everything is so beautiful down here! I could definitely see myself living here.

"Is it always like this down here?" he asks.

"Pretty much," she responds.

He turns back to face the open window, not wanting to miss a thing. He watches the tree lines blur and, suddenly, break. Through an opening in the tree lines, he sees a large marina full of large boats--from speedboats to large yachts.

They pull into a parking lot and step out. "Come on," she says. She grabs his hand and pulls him along behind her. They step onto a long dock and make their way to the very end, where the largest yacht in the marina is bobbing gently with the waves.

He follows Sissy onto the boat and up a curved staircase leading to a second level. Off to the side is a wrap-around bar, which leads to a hot tub and a pool, on the opposite end.

Damn, this thing looks expensive! I bet the dude paid at least $10 million! This is amazing!

"Carlos!" Sissy yells.

A man in his mid-thirties, dressed in blue jeans and a polo style shirt, turns around and smiles. He looks to be of European descent, with dark skin and dark-brown hair.

Sissy pulls him in the direction of the man, and he follows obediently. When they reach him, Sissy kisses the man on both cheeks and pulls back. "Carlos, this is my friend, JJ. JJ, this is Carlos. JJ is from the states. He's friends with Tanya."

Carlos eyes him with interest. "Oh, you know Tanya? How is she doing?"

"Good, staying busy," he says. "You have a beautiful yacht. Hopefully, I'll own one someday."

Carlos pulls out a business card and hands it to him. "Here, call this guy. Tell him Carlos sent you. They'll help you get a custom-built yacht whenever you're ready."

"Thank you, Sir."

Carlos laughs. "Call me Carlos, okay?"

He smiles. "Thank you, Carlos."

"Any friend of Tanya and Sissy's is a friend of mine. You two go get some drinks and get comfortable. We'll be undocking here in a few minutes," Carlos says and excuses himself.

He turns back to Sissy. "Where are we going?"

"Just a cruise around. We'll be back later tonight."

He nods and eyes the bar. "What do you want to drink? I'll get them," he says.

She flashes a flirty smile. "I will take a LONG ISLAND ICED TEA."

"Okay," he responds. He goes over to the bar and orders a LONG ISLAND ICED TEA and gets a Red Bull and vodka for himself. He returns and hands her the drink.

She thanks him and they merge into the crowd. He feels the boat shift as it leaves the dock. The wind picks up with the momentum of the boat. The cool ocean air tousles his hair, and he takes another drink.

A few hours pass before Carlos rejoins them. "Are you guys doing okay?" Carlos asks.

Sissy smiles. "Always, Carlos," she responds.

"Yeah, this is fun! Thanks for allowing me to come hang out," he says.

"No problem," Carlos responds.

"Excuse me, guys," Sissy says. "I need to use the ladies' room. I'll be back." She hands her drink to JJ and leaves them.

JJ watches her leave, scanning her backside. As soon as she's out of sight he turns back to Carlos. "So Carlos, if you don't mind me asking...where are you from?"

"Not at all. I'm originally from Holland."

"No shit! I've always wanted to visit Amsterdam."

Carlos shrugs. "Amsterdam is okay. There are other cities in Holland that are even better."

He takes a long drink. "If I ever make it to Europe, I'll have to call you and check it out!"

Carlos grins. "Yes, you do that. I'm there a lot, but I travel a lot, too." He reaches in his back pocket and pulls out his wallet. He then grabs a business card and hands it to him. "Here's my card. Give me a call and make sure I'm there, first."

"Okay, great! I will definitely call you if I go."

"So, what do you do for a living, JJ?" Carlos asks.

"I'm a chemical engineer."

Carlos raises his brows in interest. "Oh, a chemist, huh?"

"Yeah, what about you?"

"Investor. I made some good investments in some businesses that allow me the free time to play around."

...that seems scripted. He sounds like a dealer...

"That's cool. You're definitely doing well," he says, gesturing at the vessel.

Carlos chuckles. "I'm not complaining."

Sissy maneuvers her way back to JJ and reclaims her drink. "What were you guys talking about?"

"Investments," he states.

She just smiles and shakes her head. "Boys and your money."

Carlos laughs. "You're one to be talking, Sissy."

Now, Sissy laughs. "Touché, touché."

He flashes a satisfied grin and takes a step back. "I will leave you two alone," Carlos says, then turns on his heel and disappears into the sea of people.

Sissy turns back to JJ. "So, are you enjoying the night?"

"Yes, it's been great so far." He takes another mouthful, finishing his drink. "Hey, I have a question."

She gives a gentle smile. "What is it?"

"Don't take this as any disrespect, but are you single?"

She laughs, seeming relieved. "I thought you were going to say something else! But yes, I am single."

"I can't believe a beautiful girl such as yourself...and smart on top of that... is single."

"I haven't found the right guy yet. What about you?" she asks.

He grins. "Yeah, I'm single. I've just been staying focused on work."

Heavy bass pours from the speakers on the patio, vibrating the floor. "Come on, let's dance," she says.

She is so beautiful...so perfect...

They sway to the music, their bodies in sync. Her back is to him, and he can smell the sweetness of her hair. He moves his hands slowly down her side, resting them on her hips. She turns around to face him and grabs his hands. Without warning, she places his hands on her butt and wraps her arms around his neck.

Shit, I'm getting hard...cold water, think cold water. This is going to ruin the moment.

Whoa, looks like someone's enjoying this," she says, giggling.

He smiles. "What can I say? You excite me."

She gives him a mischievous smile. "Come on," she says, grabbing his hand and pulling him away.

Fuck yeah! Thank God I brought a condom with me...

He follows her across the yacht to the sleeping-cabin area. She opens a door, pulls him inside and locks it behind them.

She walks to the edge of the bed. "Sit," she says.

As he sits down, she climbs on him and starts to give him a sexy lap dance, rubbing her body all over him. She pulls his shirt off and starts kissing on him.

Man, she's good...

She kisses his neck and rubs his broad shoulders. "I love toned men," she says.

"I work out, so you'll definitely love me," he responds.

She pushes him onto his back and climbs on top of him. They continue to kiss. He grabs the bottom of her shirt, pulls it off and tosses it to the ground. He starts kissing her neck as he slowly slips her bra straps down from her shoulders and unbuttons the latch in the front.

"God, you're sexy," he says as he starts kissing the top of her chest. He slowly works his way to her breasts.

She moans when he reaches her nipples. "Damn, you're good!"

He laughs. "I try."

"Have you ever been with a Spanish girl?" she asks.

"Nope, you are my first."

"Once you have had a Latina, you always want a señorita," she says, giggling.

He smiles. "We will see."

"Trust me, you will," she moans.

While focusing his mouth on her nipples, his hands slowly slide down her stomach and unbutton her pants. She grabs ahold of his hair, but he pushes her arms up, which helps him to slide down between her legs. After getting the last four buttons undone, he grabs her pants by the waistline and pulls them, along with her black satin panties, down.

He glides slowly over her soft thighs and down to her ankles. He kisses the top of her left foot and works his way up her leg, teasing her. As he gets closer to her bald pussy, he spreads her legs. He makes his way up to her swollen clit and gives it a lick, but veers and starts kissing her right leg down to her foot.

"Oh, you're a tease," she says.

He grins. "I know."

"Come get this," she says.

She grabs him by the hair and tugs him upward. She pushes him on his back and starts rubbing his hard stomach. He tries to move, but she stops and straddles him, facing away from him. He feels her wetness drip onto his chest and hears the zipper from his pants. The next thing he feels is the soft touch of her hands around the head of his already hard and sensitive dick.

He grabs her thighs and pulls her to his face. As he starts licking her clit he feels himself go deep into her mouth as well. They continue to perform the sixty-nine position until he feels himself nearing orgasm.

"Stop...I'm going to come," he moans as he grips her thighs. She presses on, filling her mouth with his cock. His toes clench as he almost reaches orgasm, and, she stops. She turns around and smiles.

"What are you doing? I was right there," he moans.

"I know... I told you two could play that game."

He moans and pushes her to the side of the bed. "You want to play, huh?" he says. He grabs her by her ankles and pulls her to the end of the bed. He throws her legs over his shoulders and starts sucking on her clitoris. She begins gyrating her hips.

He reaches into his pocket and pulls out the condom. He digs his face deep into her pussy, freeing up both hands to open and put on the condom. "You like that?" he asks.

"Yeah...oh yeah, keep going," she moans.

He starts to kiss up her stomach. As he does, he spreads her legs, catching a glimpse of her swollen clit before he pushes himself deep inside her.

"Oh!" She lets off a loud moan and arches her back as her body accepts all of him inside her. He pushes her legs over his shoulders and begins pumping her and rubbing her clit with his thumb. "Oh shit..." she moans as she feels his head slide back and forth across her G-spot. He notices her toes start to curl.

I got her right there...

"I'm going to come," she moans as he feels her body shake. This doesn't stop him. He pumps her harder. She lets off one last sound as her body explodes and begins dripping fluid all over him.

"My turn," he moans as goes deeper. He feels her tighten her female muscles, which pushes him to climax. He drives himself deep inside her as he unloads the long-awaited orgasm into the condom inside her.

She pulls him down on top of her. "That was amazing," she says.

"No...this *is* amazing," he replies while trying to catch his breath. After a short period of relaxation, they get dressed and make their way back to the party.

"Hey, you!" a voice yells from the other side of the crowd. They watch Carlos snake through the crowd and stop in front of them. "Where have you two been? We've been looking all over for you two."

"She was just showing me around. It is extremely nice and very big. That might have been why you couldn't find us," he says.

"Why were you looking for us for?" she asks.

"I was just going to tell you that we're almost back to shore. We are going to continue the party at my place... You guys are welcome to come."

She looks at JJ. "What do you think?"

He shrugs. "Why not?"

She flashes him a smile. "Yeah, let's go."

"Sounds good!" Carlos says. "I'll be seeing you both there then?"

He nods. "We will see you there!"

After re-docking, everyone exits the yacht and makes their way back to their cars. "Man, that was fun!" he says as he slides into the passenger seat.

"Just wait--if you like the yacht, you'll love the house!" she says, closing her door.

"Really?"

"You'll see, trust me," she responds as she starts the car.

They drive with the top down and music pumping. "Do you like club music?" he yells over the wind and bass.

She turns the music down a bit, but still has to reply louder than normal. "Yes! I used to live in Ibiza, Spain!" She flips to another CD in the disc changer. "Ever heard of Sensation White in Europe?" she asks.

"Hell yeah! All the top DJs play that! Have you been there?"

"Yeah! That party was the shit! This is a live mix from it!"

DJ Tiesto's music starts playing over the speakers. "Shit! It's DJ Tiesto! I've always wanted to see him live!" he says.

She smiles. "Next time I go to Sensation White, you're more than welcome to join me," she says in a girly voice, placing her hand on his thigh.

"Fuck yeah! I'm there!"

She pulls into a long driveway and parks along the side of the smooth pavement. He gets out and looks at what he considers the dictionary definition of a mansion.

Damn, this house is huge!

Sissy sees his expression and grins. "So, what do you think?"

"This place is enormous!" he says.

She laughs. "Come on, let's go look around… and then you can see for yourself!"

They get out and walk up to the front door. A man in a plain-colored polo greets them. "Come inside," he says with a smile. The main entrance is packed with people and loud music.

"This house is awesome!" he says.

Carlos sees them enter and heads over. "Glad you guys made it!"

She smiles. "Thanks for inviting us."

He looks at Carlos and nods. "Yes, Carlos, thank you! Your house is amazing! If you ever want to sell it, let me know! I'd give you my left nut to get it," he says, laughing.

Carlos smiles. "I'll keep that in mind." He turns to Sissy. "Everyone is out back, but you can take him to explore if you like."

"Okay, thanks, Dear," Sissy replies. She grabs his hand and leads him around the opposite side of the house and through a side door.

He's amazed by the architecture and the amount of space this house

contains.

The design is so amazing! Five bedrooms, five-and-a-half baths, two

kitchens and a master bedroom with a view!

As they stand looking at the ocean, he looks down at the crowd.

"This place has a large outdoor living space *and* a pool with swim-up

bar! All it needs is a movie theater, and you'd never have to leave!" he

says.

Sissy smiles and laughs. "It's down the hall!"

He looks at her. "I want this house."

She just smiles. "Maybe Carlos will sell it."

"I do hope so... I really want this house!" he says, laughing.

"Come on, let's go to the party," she says as she grabs his hand and

pulls him behind her.

They go down by the pool and find an empty beach chair. He sits,

and Sissy joins him happily. He watches some of the women strip down

to only panties and jump in the pool. "These people party like this all

the time?" he asks.

She looks down at him from her place on his lap. "All the time," she replies, taking a drink from the beer he's holding.

He sits back in the chair. *I love this place... I think I want to live here...*

QUICK

He wakes up, images of the previous night still fresh in his head. He remembers the instructions Tanya gave him before they went to sleep. He grabs Papi's throwaway phone and calls Marco.

Set up meeting...act like Papi...be fast on your toes...can't let Marco figure out what's up...

"Hello, Papi," Marco answers.

He keeps his voice low, and replies. "Hello, Marco."

"I hope you have good news."

"I do, but I'd like to talk in person."

There's a pause before Marco responds. "Okay, stop by now, then."

He's caught off guard momentarily, but he knows he has to stick to Tanya's plan. "I'm busy right now, but I'm going to be on the boat tonight--meet me there. I'll leave the door open."

"The family boat?" Marco asks.

"Yes, I was planning to get some strippers and hang out for a while... Are you in?"

There's another pause before Marco answers. "Why not? We need to talk anyways."

"Alright, good, because if you weren't coming, I would just have more for myself," Quick responds.

"What time?" Marco asks.

"Let's say 11:00 tonight."

"Okay," Marco says. "I will see you at the boat at 11:00."

"Okay, see you then," he replies, then hangs up. He immediately calls Tanya.

"Did you call him?" she answers.

"Damn, Cousin, hello to you, too."

"Sorry...hello, Quick, good morning. How are you?"

He laughs. "That's better...but yes, I did. He's going to meet us on the family boat tonight at 11:00. I told him I was getting strippers, so you figure out how to draw him into the boat. I told him the door would be open."

"Okay, good work, Quick. Make sure you meet up with me and Smurf today at the restaurant, and we'll go over everything," she says.

"Okay, I'll be down there at lunchtime," he replies.

"Okay, we'll meet you down there" she responds

"Okay see you soon" Quick responds and ends the call.

Fuck the Guzman's! We'll kill them one at a time if we have to...

MARCO

After hanging up the call with Papi, Marco sits back in his chair.

That's strange...every time Papi and I meet, it's always at a neutral location... now, he wants me to meet at the Zaragosa family boat?...

The butterfly feeling in his stomach makes him sick. He knows that every time he gets a gut feeling, it's usually right. Now, he has a feeling that Papi is setting him up.

I knew I couldn't trust that Colombian piece of shit!

He picks up his phone and calls Roberto. "Yes, boss," Roberto answers.

"Roberto, where are you?"

"Just pulling up to the grocery store."

"Okay good, see you in a few minutes," he replies and disconnects. He takes a few sips from his drink as he waits for Roberto to walk through the door.

It doesn't take long before the office door swings open and Roberto steps through. "What did you need?" he asks, closing the door behind him.

"Papi called," he says.

"Good news?" Roberto asks.

"He said he wants to meet at the docks tonight at 11:00PM. I'm busy, so I need you and a couple of guys to go meet him on the Zaragosa boat."

Roberto nods. "Alright."

"Make sure you keep your eyes and ears open. If something doesn't seem right, back away."

"You think he's setting us up?"

He shakes his head. "Not for sure, but you know how I feel about that family."

"I understand… They're greedy Colombians," Roberto replies.

"Now, if something happens, you call me ASAP, okay?"

"Yes, Boss, I will let you know what happens."

He nods. "Okay, get some men together and remember: Meet at the Zaragosa boat at 11:00PM and call to let me know what happens."

"Got it," Roberto says.

"Okay, good, now get to work." Roberto turns and leaves the office. The door latches shut, and Marco is alone again. The butterfly feeling in his stomach is growing in intensity.

Not this time, Papi…not this time

TANYA

"Who was that, T?" Smurf asks.

"It was Quick. He is going to meet us at the restaurant during lunch. He set up the meeting for tonight, on the boat at 11:00PM."

"So, what's the plan?" Smurf asks.

"Well, Quick told Marco that he was having strippers there, so we need to make it look and sound legit."

"What do you have in mind?"

"Well, I figure if we leave some bras sitting around for him to see, and if he hears music, he'll walk his ass right into it."

"What if he has people with him?"

"Well, we're going to keep Quick in the parking lot with a walkie-talkie to let us know, but I figure if he walks in, we secure his ass, tie him up and take his ass out into the middle of Lake Michigan...cement his feet and toss his ass overboard." Smurf laughs. "What? I want him to suffer like he's made me, and what's better than dying slowly? We're going to need some quick cement and some buckets."

Smurf stops laughing long enough to ask, "Are you serious?"

"As serious as heart attack," she says.

He smiles. "That's why I love you, Ma. Crazy and sexy...and just a straight badass!"

"Well, I don't play when it comes to me and this family. I'll make it a point to destroy the Guzmans." Smurf rolls over on their bed and kisses her neck. "Hey, hey, hey...later. Let's take on this first," she says as she kisses him softly on the lips. She rolls out of bed. "Get ready," she says.

I can't wait to see his face as we toss his ass into the water...

She's at the office in the restaurant with Smurf. Every detail for tonight has been thought through and set up. No slip-ups.

There's a knock at the door, and Quick steps in. "Hello?"

"What's up, Family?" Smurf says.

"Hey, Quick, come and sit down," she says, pointing to the empty seat.

Quick scoots the chair closer to the desk and sits. "So, what's up, Tanya?"

"For this to work, we need you to keep point in the parking lot. If he shows up and isn't alone, we need to know what we're dealing with. We're going to have walkie-talkies, so you can just beep and tell us," she says.

"What if he does have people with him?" Quick asks.

"Let us know how many, and if we need help, you're going to get him running, you feel me?"

Quick smiles. "Yeah, it would be a pleasure to shoot at them stupid Guzmans."

"We only have one shot at this, so it's *got* to count."

"What time are we planning to meet up for this?"

"We need to get there early, just in case," she says. "So let's say 9:45PM, but meet at the condo at 9:00PM."

"Okay, I'll be at the crib at 9:00PM...anything else?"

She shakes her head. "No, Smurf and I will take care of the rest."

"Okay, well, I need to take care of some things. I will meet you guys at 9."

"Alright, Quick," she says.

"Later, Family," Smurf says.

Quick gets up and leaves. "See ya," he says before closing the door.

Smurf turns back to Tanya. "So, what do we need to do?"

"We'll need walkie-talkies, and I need you to go and get some metal buckets and quick cement. Drop it all off at the boat. Oh, and we need some duct tape and rope to tie Marco's bitch ass up."

"Okay, I will run to the home improvement store and get all that. Are you going to stay here for a minute, or do you need a ride back to the house?" he asks.

"I will stay here. Just come back after you're done and get me."

"Okay, T, I will be back in a bit," he says and kisses her.

"Okay, I will see you later."

As soon as Smurf leaves, she starts to call other family members in other states. She calls the family heads in each state and tells them about Papi's abandonment of the family. She tells them that both she and Smurf are now the main contacts for the family.

With Papi gone, I have three times the work to do...

This process of calling takes several hours. She finishes just as Smurf returns. "You took care of all that?" she asks.

"Yes, I dropped it off."

"Good...I can't wait to see his face tonight," she says with a grin.

"I can tell," he replies.

"I've waited patiently for this day to come, Smurf. The pain has been horrible." He walks over and starts rubbing her shoulders. She moans, "That feels good." She starts to relax a little.

"Come on, let's go home," he says.

"Alright, I'm done here anyways." As they head to Smurf's car, thoughts flood her head. She goes over every detail of the plan, imagining different scenarios.

This has to work... Just one kink will mess this whole thing up...

They arrive at the condo and she checks the clock in the kitchen. It's 5:00PM, and they still have four hours until Quick gets there.

"What do you want to do?" Smurf asks.

She shrugs. "Just chill out, I guess."

"Okay, go kick back and find a movie. You hungry?" he asks. She nods. "Okay, I'll make something."

"Alright," she replies. She goes into the living room and snuggles up with a pillow. The same thoughts that have been running through her mind continue, making it impossible to relax.

Why am I so nervous? I'm a professional killer...

Smurf comes into the living room with a couple plates and a bag of chips. She sees he's made some sandwiches and smiles as he sits down beside her.

Knock, knock, knock.

Smurf sighs, but gets up and answers the door. When he opens the door, Quick is standing in front of him. "What's up, Family?" Smurf asks.

"What's up, Smurf?" Quick replies as he walks into the living room. "Do you have 'em? The walkie-talkies?"

Smurf nods and goes to the other room. He returns with three walkie-talkies and hands one to Quick. "Here...now, what we need is you to be our eyes and ears when Marco shows. We don't want to be caught off guard, alright?"

"That's it?" Quick asks.

Tanya jumps in. "Well, if we get into trouble and need help, your ass better come running...but we need him to be alone."

Quick nods. "Okay, I'll see what I can do."

She turns to Smurf. "Now, Smurf, I need you to be at the controls, because once he gets inside, I plan on hitting his ass with the butt of my gun, and we need to get away from shore in case he tries to yell for help. We got one chance to do this."

"With Marco out of the way, we will run through the rest of the family... and then the city will be ours," Quick says.

"Exactly," she replies.

"No competition," Smurf says with a smirk. He checks the clock in the kitchen. "Well it's getting close to the deadline time... We better get going."

"Yeah, let's go," she says. She grabs a bag from the next room before they all leave. They pile into the rental car that Quick has been driving and head to the docks.

"Everyone got a walkie-talkie?" she asks from the passenger seat.

"Yes, T," Smurf says. Quick grabs his from his jacket and shakes it for her.

"Okay, everyone go to Channel five," she says. She turns hers on. "Test, test..." The echoes come from the other walkie-talkies.

They arrive and park in the lot, close enough to have a good view of the walkway to the marina..

"Now, remember, Quick, tell us when he gets here and if anyone is with him," she says.

"I know, I will," Quick says.

"Okay, come on, Smurf," she says as she gets out. They walk up the dock towards the family boat. On board, she leaves the door to the living area unlocked.

"So, what's the plan?" Smurf asks.

"I'm going to toss a couple of bras on the outside deck to draw him in. Once he's inside, I'm going to hit his ass in the head with my gun and yell 'go.' You take off."

"What if he's got people with him?"

"Fuck it. Kill them," she says in an angry tone.

"You're the boss," Smurf says and walks away.

She walks over to the stereo system and turns on some music, then goes to drop the bras around the outside of the boat.

"Hey, I'm going to unhook us from the dock," Smurf says.

"Okay, we need to be ready." He leaves again, and she grabs her walkie-talkie. "Quick," she says into the speaker.

She hears a beep, followed by Quick's voice. "Yeah, still nothing... We still got ten minutes."

"Okay, let us know."

Another beep. "No problem, Cousin."

Finally...I'll avenge my father and my brother's deaths...

A beep brings her back. "Hey...hey, they're here!" Quick says.

"On the dock yet?" she asks.

"Not yet."

Smurf jumps into the radio conversation. "How many?"

"Three."

Shit, three of them...

"Hey, they're coming your way now," Quick says.

"All of them?" she asks.

"Yes."

"Okay Quick, keep an eye on us. We might need help."

"Alright, I'm moving now."

"Smurf, can you see them yet?" she asks.

"Yes, three of them...but one is hanging back."

"Be ready to move. One's getting shot," she says as she sits in the corner.

Father, keep me safe...

She takes a deep breath as the first man enters. It's not Marco. As the second man enters, she fires a shot into the back of the first man. She slams the butt of her gun into the side of the second man's head, knocking him down. The jolts from the sudden acceleration cause the boat to sway, and she loses her footing. After regaining her balance, she fires another shot into the first man's back.

Quick comes over the speaker again. "That nigga is running for the parked car!"

"Don't let him get away!" she yells. She turns over and sees the second man.

It's not Marco... Fuck, it's not him! Shit! MotherFucker!"

She yells into her walkie-talkie again. "Quick, keep your eye on the other guy!"

"I am! He's just hanging!"

"Smurf, come to me! I need your help down here!" she yells. The hum of the engine calms, letting her know that Smurf is on his way.

He rushes into the living area. "What's up? You get him?" Smurf asks.

"It's not him," she says.

"What?" He walks to her. "Who was it?"

"It's fucking Roberto! His right hand! Marco must have known something was up."

Anger and disappointment wash over Smurf's face. "Fuck it...we'll get Marco, T...but we'll get this dude now." He helps drag Roberto to a chair and tie him up.

They wait for Roberto to wake up. As he comes to consciousness, he notices the rope and duct tape.

"Look who it is...Marco's bitch-boy, Roberto. So nice to see you," she says, smiling.

Roberto glares at her. "Marco was right about tonight."

"Yeah? That's too bad," she says sarcastically. "I really wanted to kill him, not you...but you'll have to do for now." She turns around to discuss how she wants things done.

As she talks to Smurf, Roberto sees what Smurf has already begun doing. His partner's dead body lays on the floor with his feet in a metal bucket. Smurf is pouring some sort of cement mixture into the bucket. Roberto knows this isn't going to end well.

In a state of adrenaline-fueled desperation, Roberto looks at Smurf. "You must be Tanya's bitch...Smurf...I've heard a lot about you."

Smurf gets up. "I got your bitch, Family" He leaves the room.

Roberto looks at Tanya. "You just signed your own death warrant."

"How so?" she asks.

"If I don't live, Marco will know this was a set up... Then you, Papi, and that nigga of yours is dead!"

She smiles. "Well, no worries on Papi's end... he's already dead."

Smurf returns with a fillet knife. "I'll show you bitch!" he yells. He slices the upper part of Roberto's face, and blood spills into his eyes and mouth. Roberto screams.

"Where's Marco!" she yells over his wails.

Roberto grits his teeth. "Fuck you and your family!"

Smurf starts to fillet both his cheeks; the screams echo in the room.

"Where is Marco!" she yells again.

Roberto spits blood at Tanya. She wipes the blood from her arm. "Fuck this! Smurf, get his feet."

Smurf walks behind him and hits him with his gun, knocking Roberto out. They untie him from the chair and bind his wrists with duct tape. They lay him next to the dead man and cement his feet into another metal bucket.

She waits until the cement is mostly dry before yelling, "Wake up! Wake up, MotherFucker!" She slaps him for good measure. As he starts to come around again she calls Marco from Roberto's phone.

"What happened?" Marco answers.

"Oh, I'm sorry, were you looking for Roberto? He's a little tied up right now," she says.

Marco can hear the glee in her voice at these words. "Tanya, you hood rat! You're dead!" he yells.

She laughs. "Stop that, you're making me blush. Roberto wants to say something to you." She places the phone to Roberto's ear.

Roberto is barely conscious, but gives her one final glare. "Kill her!" he yells. Tanya puts a bullet in the back of Roberto's head.

Marco hears the gunshot from the other end. "Roberto!"

"Did you enjoy that, Marco?" she asks.

"I'm going to kill you, Tanya! And your whole family! You're going to pay for this!" Marco yells.

"I'll be waiting," she replies.

"You're going to be seeing your piece-of-shit father and brother soon! Real soon, Tanya!"

"Goodbye, Marco," she replies, then makes a kiss sound into the phone before disconnecting. She turns to Smurf. "Toss their bodies."

Smurf drags Roberto and tosses him into the water, followed by the other dead man. "What about the boat?" he asks.

"Fuck it. Blow it up--make it look like an accident," she says. Smurf nods. She gets on her walkie-talkie. "Quick?"

A beep. "Hey, Cousin," he says, catching his breath.

"Where are you?"

"Fuck, Cousin...I was chasing that dude, but I lost him."

"It's okay, let him go. Get the car ready. We're leaving in less than five."

"Okay, I will be ready," he replies.

She turns back to Smurf. "Take care of this, then meet me at the car." She steps off the boat and heads back to the car.

Quick is waiting for her, the engine running. She gets in the passenger seat and closes the door.

"Where's Smurf?" Quick asks.

"He's coming, just wait."

Smurf shows up after a few minutes. "Let's go," he says, and hops in the back seat.

As they speed down the street, a loud boom goes off from outside. It sounds like a bomb echoing in the air from behind them. She turns around to see a large cloud of fire and smoke rising from the marina. She looks at Smurf. He just smiles and shrugs his shoulders. She smiles and turns back, facing forward in the seat.

Marco...I got your bitch ass next time.

.

GEORGE (a few months later)

It's late, and he's working in the lab. They've been so backed up, he's been putting in extra time to compensate. His resentment towards JJ is growing.

This guy just thinks he can come and go as he pleases. Ever since his weekend vacation a few months ago, he expects me to do all the work. Thank God Quick has learned what I've taught him, so he can at least help around here...

His thoughts and work are interrupted by the large metal door opening. He looks up and sees JJ walking in. "Thanks for coming," he says in a smartass tone.

JJ walks up to him at the lab table.

"What is your problem?" JJ asks.

George begins to laugh. "Seriously? You don't know?"

"Enlighten me," JJ says.

"Well, first off, you piss me off with how you just come and go around here. We're a team, jackass, yet I can't ever find you on the weekend, and barely do during the week. Thank God Quick has learned how to help, or this shit would never get made."

JJ laughs. "That's bullshit. And you know what, George? Fuck, I could make this alone."

"So? I know you can do it, too. Well, ever since you went on that vacation, you're never around. What the hell are you doing?" he asks.

"What's it matter to you?" JJ responds.

"Well, it must be important to leave me hanging. So, what is it?"

"If you must know, I've been visiting a female."

"She better be Miss Universe, because I'm sick of the bullshit around here. While you're out playing around, I'm here working long hours."

Quick walks into the lab and catches them arguing.

"Then, fucking quit, George! Nobody's keeping you here!" JJ yells.

"Whoa, whoa, what's going on?" Quick says as he jumps between them.

"JJ wants to make his own hours," George says.

"So, I may work how I want George, Hell I can do this alone!" JJ yells back.

"Come on, guys, relax. What the fuck?" Quick argues.

"I'm sick of the bullshit, JJ. I'm sick of you!" George yells.

"Hey, George, relax. You've been working hard... Maybe you need a break," Quick says.

"This shit has been building for some time. While JJ, here, is out playing around, I'm stuck in the lab slaving away making product.

"I can't enjoy my money? What's the point of having it?" JJ yells.

"Fuck this!" George yells back, throwing his arms up.

"You do that, you little baby," JJ replies as he acts as if he's wiping tears from his eyes.

He charges JJ and hits him with a right jab. "Wipe this off your eyes!" he yells, as he tackles JJ to the ground. They start rolling on the floor, fighting. Quick tries to break it up, but is unsuccessful.

They continue to roll around as each one of them throws punches wildly, they finally piss Quick off enough, so that Quick pulls out his gun and fires a shot off. "Stop!" Quick yells. The two of them come to a standstill. "Get up, both of you," he yells again. They both stand up. "Now, both of you are going to figure this shit out. We have enough drama already--we don't need anymore!"

"I'm sorry, JJ," says George.

"Me too," JJ replies.

"Are we good?" Quick asks.

"Yeah, but I'm taking the rest of the day off," George says.

"Yeah, do that. JJ and I got this. Go home and relax," Quick says to him. George grabs his keys and heads to his car, parked out back.

After leaving, and stopping by to get some food, George ends up at his place. While eating his food, his phone rings. It's his mother.

"Hi, Mom," he answers.

"Jesus, George, what have you been doing?!" She's frantic on the other end.

"Mom, calm down. What are you talking about?"

"The police in Ames called, looking for you!"

"What for?" he asks.

"A murder, George. They said someone named Mark is dead."

"What? Mark is dead?! I didn't even know he died!"

"Well, the police seem to think you did it George. If you didn't do it, you need to get your ass back here and turn yourself in," she begins yelling, then continues to rant about other issues.

"Okay, okay, okay. I will leave tomorrow. I'll turn myself in." He ends the call and sits back on the couch.

Can it get any worse? How am I going to tell Mindy?...

MINDY

She pulls into the parking lot of George's place and grabs the sack from the passenger seat. She's packed a few movies and a bottle of wine.

I hope he likes surprises!

She smiles mischievously to herself and gets out of her car. She makes her way up to George's door and quietly unlocks it. As she's closing the door behind her, she hears George talking.

"What for?... What? Mark is dead?! I didn't even know he died!.... Okay, okay, okay. I will leave tomorrow. I'll turn myself in."

Her heart stops as she catches her breath. This is a surprise she definitely didn't want.

Without a sound, she opens the door and leaves.

TANYA

Ring, ring.

"What's up, Mindy?" Tanya answers.

"Where are you?" Mindy asks.

"I'm at home. Are you okay?"

"We have a problem."

"I'll be there soon. Don't leave, alright?"

"I'll be here," she replies, then hangs up.

What now? Always one thing, then another.

When Mindy shows up, she wastes no time. "Tanya, we got a problem."

"What is it?" Tanya asks.

"It's George. I went to his place to see him because he and JJ got into a fight earlier. I walked into his house, and he was on the phone."

"Okay," she says.

"I overheard the call. That Mark guy I took care of for JJ back in Iowa..."

"Yeah, what about him?"

"They think George had something to do with it."

"Shit. What's he planning on doing?"

"He said he was going to turn himself in tomorrow."

She sits back, closes her eyes and then slams her fist down on the table.

Fuck, he knows too much about our family. He would destroy us, all of us.

Mindy starts to cry. She rubs Mindy's back. "We can't risk it, Honey."

"I know, I know," she says through tears.

"Are you going to be able to do this?" she asks Mindy. "I can get someone else to do it."

"No, I will do it. I just wish I didn't have to."

"Me too, Honey, me too," she replies, while still rubbing Mindy's back.

"How do you want it done?" Mindy asks.

"Take him on vacation. Enjoy your last few days together. Just make sure you do it, Mindy. You feel me?" replies Tanya.

"I understand you. I'm not stupid, Tanya. Just in love."

"Which can blur your sense of reality, and the reality is, he could put us all away forever. We can't have that now, can we?"

"I know; I'll take care of it," Mindy says as she stands up. "I got to go."

"Okay, let me know. I love you, Mindy."

"I love you too, cousin," Mindy replies.

Mindy leaves, and she sits back in her chair.

Please Mindy, don't fuck this up...

JJ

While at the lab, he pulls the card out that Carlos had given him on his vacation down in Los Cabos.

I wonder what type of boats this place has. I bet they aren't cheap eithe...Elite Yachts Corp.

He enters the website link from the card into Internet Explorer and hits enter. After being sent to the company's home page, he begins to look through the links to different boats. He stumbles upon an eighty-five-foot yacht.

Damn, this thing comes with a helicopter and heliport!

He scrolls down and finds the price: Three million dollars.

"JJ, come here!" Quick yells.

Okay, I'm coming," he says as he adds the site to his internet favorites, and then makes his way over to Quick.

"What's up?"

"Hey, did I do this right? Did I mix this correctly?" Quick asks.

"Tell me what you did step-by-step."

"Okay," Quick replies as he starts to go into detail of each step he performed in the formula.

"Well, you're doing it all right. Actually, exactly on the money. You're pretty good... You just learned from George?"

"Yes, he asked me to help while you were gone."

"Well, you've learned fast. Chemistry is great to know, because the world will always need a chemist. Keep up the good work. If you need me, just yell. I'm going to get back on the computer."

"Okay, thanks, JJ. Hey, Man, are you and George really okay now?" Quick asks.

"Yeah, just, sometimes I don't get him. I want to enjoy my money, you know what I mean?"

"I feel you, JJ. So, it's in the past, but get back to work, alright?"

An hour passes as he plays on the Internet, searching for stuff during there down time waiting for chemical reactions.

Ring, ring.

He picks up his cell, but doesn't recognize the number on the screen.

"Hello?"

"Hello, JJ."

"Who's this?" he asks.

"It's Carlos. I got your number from Sissy."

"Oh, what's up, Bro?" JJ asks.

"Nothing too much. I don't know if Sissy told you, but I just got a good deal on a new place down here. And I remember you saying you were interested in my house."

"Yes, what are you trying to get for it?"

"I'll give it to you for $2.25 million, and I will even sell my Ferrari 360 and a Lamborghini Diablo VT. I upgrade every few years anyways."

"Dang, that's a steal! Let me see what I can do. I will call you back."

"Okay, let me know."

"I will. Thanks for letting me know, Carlos."

"No problem, but I got another call. Let me know what you're going to do."

"I will talk to you soon," he replies and hangs up. He dials Sissy's number.

"Hello?" she says.

"Are you just waking up, Sissy?"

"Yes," she moans.

"Carlos just called."

"Yeah, I gave him your number. I hope you don't mind."

"It's okay."

"So, are you going to buy it?" she asks.

"Well, that's my problem. I got the money, but I can't move it, at least not all of it at once."

"How much does he want?"

"$2.25 million."

"Damn, that's a deal. He got it for $3 million when he first got down here."

"Yeah I know; it's a steal."

"I'll tell you what, I will take care of Carlos. You give the money to Tanya and tell her it's for me. She'll make sure I get it."

"Seriously, Sissy? You'll do that?"

"Yeah, I will."

"Okay, thank you! I have to call Carlos.

"No, don't worry about him. I will call him. Just get ahold of Tanya."

"I'm going to find her now."

"I will let you go then," Sissy replies.

"Alright, I will talk to you later," he responds, then hangs up. JJ then walks to where Quick is working.

JJ asks, "Hey, do you know where Tanya is?"

"Nope, just call her phone," Quick replies.

He dials in Tanya's number and calls.

"Hello?" she answers.

"Hello, Tanya."

"What's up, JJ?

"Nothing too much. Hey, are you free to talk in person?"

"Well, I'm pretty busy today. How about tomorrow?"

"Sure, what time?" he responds.

"Let's meet at George and Mindy's place at noon. Will that work?" she asks.

"Yes, I'll see you there at noon tomorrow."

"Sounds good. I'll see you then. Sorry, I got to cut it short," she says.

"No problem. I will see you tomorrow."

"Okay, see you," she replies and hangs up.

JJ and Quick continue to work on a batch of Bliss. His phone rings, and he looks to see who it is.

It's Amy. "Hello?"

"JJ?"

"Yeah, Amy. What's up? I'm kind of in the middle of something."

"It's Mark."

"Hold on one second," he replies as he distances himself from Quick and sneaks into another room.

"Okay, now, what about Mark?"

"He's dead."

"What? What do you mean dead?"

"He was gunned down in his house."

"They have any leads?" JJ asks.

"Well, the cops talked to me, and I guess George was with him the day before his death, so they think he did it. They are trying to find him to talk to him about it."

Shit, if they get to him, it'll ruin everything. He knows too much...

"Hello? JJ?"

"I'm here; that's crazy about Mark. Sorry to hear about it. He must have really pissed someone off."

"Well, I'm calling you to give you the heads up on what's going on down here."

"Thank you, Amy. How's everything down there? Busy?"

"Business is very busy."

"Good to hear," he replies.

"Thank you, JJ, for everything."

"It's cool, just keep with it and check in periodically. Let me know how things are going, okay?"

"Okay, I will, but hey, Amy, I have to run. Let me know if you hear anything else, for sure."

"I will. I will talk to you later," she replies.

"Okay, see you soon," he says back, then hangs up.

He dials George's number right away. He waits impatiently for an answer.

"Hello?" George answers.

"Where are you?"

"I'm at home. Why?"

"Did you hear about Mark?"

"What did you hear?" George asks.

"He was gunned down."

George begins to stumble as he speaks, nothing coherent making its way from his lips.

"Come down to the warehouse. We need to talk now," JJ says.

"Fine, I'll be there in twenty minutes."

"Okay, see you in twenty," JJ says, then hangs up.

He walks back over to watch Quick work on the Bliss.

"Everything cool, JJ?"

"Yeah, just a little kink in the chain, but I got it fixed."

It's exactly twenty minutes later when George walks through the large metal door. "Hey, JJ. Let's talk."

The two of them walk into a small office and sit at a table.

"How did you hear about Mark?" George asks him.

"Amy just called me. She even told me the police are looking for you."

"They think I killed him. I didn't do it," George replies.

"I told you not to mess with him if he got out, and you did it anyways."

"Yeah, so?"

"So, the mother fucker was probably trying to build a case on us, Bro. Did he ever ask for anything drug wise?"

"No, why would he do that to us? We are his friends," George says in defense.

"It doesn't matter. That shit is out the window once you're in handcuffs. One of your best friends working with police to get less time, so don't think because he was our friend he wouldn't do it, because that was exactly what he was doing all this time."

"This just too much for me to process right now," George says, as he rubs his temples with his fingers.

"Who told you, George?"

"My mom... She called yelling that I'm wanted for murder."

"So, what are you going to do, Bro?" JJ asks.

"I told my mom I would turn myself in."

"What the fuck?" JJ yells. "You're not going to do it, right?"

"I didn't kill Mark!" George yells, slamming his fists on a desk.

"Relax, Bro. Why are you going to turn yourself in if you didn't do it? That's stupid."

"So, what then? Go on the run?"

"Just for a minute, until they let it blow over."

"Well, Mindy did want to go on vacation."

"Yeah, do that! Get away and relax for a bit."

"I can't believe this shit! Why me?" George asks, exasperated.

"Shit happens, Bro. Can't stop it."

"What about the Bliss?"

"I got it covered. Just go relax for a while, Bro."

"You're right, that's what I'm going to do. Take a relaxing getaway for a bit."

"Good, don't worry about this. It will blow over in time. You and Mindy go have fun, wherever you decide to go.

"Okay, I'm going to go see Mindy. Thanks, JJ."

"Yup, no big deal, George," he replies. They get up, walk out of the office and JJ escorts George out the door. He closes it, then turns around then leans up against it.

Man...I have to tell Tanya about this.

TANYA

"Hey, are you two almost ready? Your flight is at 2:00PM this afternoon, and you have to be there an hour early!" she yells at Mindy.

"Almost ready!" Mindy yells back from her room.

Knock, knock.

She gets up and answers the door. "JJ, come in."

"Hey, thanks for seeing me."

"No problem, but before we talk, we need to get Mindy and George to the airport for that vacation."

"Yes, where to?" he asks.

"Not sure," George replies from the couch. "Mindy is surprising me."

"That's good, you need a vacation."

Mindy enters the room from the back bedroom. "Okay, I'm ready to go. Are you ready yet?"

"I'm ready," George says, flashing her a smile.

Mindy smiles and turns to JJ. "Hey, JJ, will you keep an eye on the house while we're gone?"

JJ nods. "I will. So, Mindy, you're surprising George?"

"Yeah, but he'll love it," Mindy says with a smile.

"Let's get going," Tanya says to everyone.

After leaving the condo, they end up in the parking lot. "I got a rental," she says as she walks to a BMW SUV. They load the luggage and hop in.

"Well, you guys enjoy it. Spend some money, George. You've earned it," JJ says.

"Thanks, JJ," George replies as they come to a stop outside the airport. Everyone gets out and says their goodbyes.

As Tanya hugs Mindy, she whispers in her ear, "Don't forget."

Mindy just nods. "I love you, Cousin."

"I love you, too, Mindy," she replies.

Mindy and George walk into the airport and out of Tanya's sight. JJ and her climb back into the BMW.

"So, what did you need to talk about?" she asks.

"Well, two things," he replies. "First, I don't know if you heard, but George is wanted for questioning on a possible murder back home. I figured, we are all together, so you should know.

"Yes, I know about the questioning. Mindy informed me. What was the other?"

"Oh, well, I wanted to see if you could help me out with Carlos, your friend from Los Cabos. He called and told me he was selling his house."

"The one with this swim-up bar in the pool?" she asks.

"Yeah, that one. He wants $ 2.25 million for it, now. I have the funds to buy it, but no way to get the money to him. So, I called Sissy, and she said she'll take care of it and to just give my money to you, and you will get the money to her."

"I can do that, it's no problem."

"She's a cool-ass chick," JJ says.

"Yeah, her and I go way back," Tanya replies.

"Yeah, she told me, way back to the old country...but you'll do that for me?"

"Yes, I got you. We all need to go party down there."

"That sounds like a plan to me," JJ says with a smile.

"Hey, you're not busy, are you, JJ? I need to stop by the mall super quick."

"No, I'm free."

"Okay, good," she replies.

"What do you need to go to the mall for, anyways?"

"I bought a shirt and, when I got home, I didn't like it. So, I'm taking it back."

He begins to laugh. "Typical female," he says with a smile.

She laughs. "Shut up, JJ. We're here; let's go get this done real quick."

After getting out of the car and grabbing the shirt, they walk into the mall. Tanya walks towards the store, passing by the food court.

"Hey, Tanya, you thirsty?" JJ asks.

"Actually, yes, I am."

"Okay, I'm going to get us something to drink."

"Okay, I'll be over here," she replies and points to the store nearby.

As JJ walks off into the food court, she makes her way to the register. After being helped, she waits for the girl behind the counter to return from the back room. In an instant, she feels a large object pressing into her back.

"Head forward, you stupid, Colombian bitch. Turn, and I'll put two hollow points in you right here."

"What do you want?" she asks.

"We've waited a long time to finally catch you slipping. Now, it's

251

our turn to pay you back for Roberto," the man says from behind her.

Fuck, after all this time, I finally slipped up. One time...

The man jabs her with the gun.

"What the--"

"Stop talking, Bitch. Let's take a walk," he interjects. He pushes her

out of the store and into the mall.

This is it, the end of me and the Zaragosa crime family.

JJ

I hope she likes Pepsi... That's all they had..."

He walks towards the store where Tanya was waiting, with two plastic cups. He notices her walking with someone.

Who is that black dude? That isn't Smurf...

As he gets closer, he notices the man has a pistol to her back. Realization floods over him, and he has to think fast. He ducks into a corner jewelry store and hides behind a case. When Tanya and the man walk by, he gets up slow, then goes into the Sprint store.

"Yo, Homie!" he yells to draw the man's attention. When the man takes his eyes off Tanya, he tackles him to the ground, pushing Tanya down, as well. As soon as the dude hits the ground, his gun slides under a bench near them. The black man and JJ fight, rolling around on the ground. JJ hits the man with his right elbow, and then with a left jab, but the man keeps coming. The man rolls over and starts beating on him. He tries to get free, but can't.

A yell from a female bystander rings out through the chaos. "She's got a gun!"

This cry catches JJ and the dude off guard. The man stops hitting JJ, and he looks up to see Tanya, standing behind the man.

"Let him up, let him up!" Tanya yells. "Your ass has been touched by an angel, Nigga, but don't worry, Smoke Jr. and I will be seeing you again real soon."

Smurf scrambles up. "Come on, let's blow this popsicle stand!"

The two of them take off running through the mall and out to the SUV. They hurry to get out of the mall parking lot.

"Who was that?" he asks.

"His name is Smoke Jr. He works for our competition."

"I guess they just tried to kill you," he says.

"Yes, but you saved me. And for that, I thank you. Have you ever shot a gun?" she asks.

"A few times."

"Here, then, take this one," she says as she hands him Smoke's Desert Eagle. She then says, "Welcome to the family."

"I need this?" he asks.

"You definitely need a pistol in this family. That's yours now."

"Thanks," he responds as he inspects the gun.

"Now, let's get your new house taken care of," she says. He stays silent and nods in agreement.

I just got myself into deep trouble...

He sits back and places the gun on his lap.

TANYA

While at the restaurant taking care of the money for JJ, Smurf shows up.

"T. Hey, Honey."

"What? Good thing you came. I need to talk to you."

"Everything okay?" Smurf asks.

"Well, JJ and I had a run in with Smoke today."

"What? Where?"

"The mall," she replies

"What happened?"

"JJ and I dropped off Mindy and George at the airport. Then, I needed to take back a shirt I didn't like at the mall, so I returned it. Well, JJ went to the food court to get us some drinks and, before I knew it, I had a gun jammed into my back."

"That mother fucker. I'm going to kill his ass!" Smurf yells.

"JJ saved my life. He ended up jumping Smoke, allowing me to get his gun. Smoke lucked out, because if it wasn't for the whistle-blowing bitch that yelled, 'she's got a gun,' I would've smoked his ass right there in the mall."

Smurf just shakes his head. "This shit can't happen again, T."

"I know, I know. They caught me slipping once, but won't twice. I'm going to bump security up around me. They got way too close for comfort this time. Never again."

"Good, because if I lose you…"

"We are not even going to think like that," she says. "Just be prepared, Smurf," she responds. "I know, I will be. They aren't catching me slipping twice."

SMOKE JR (Two days after the mall event)

Smoke Jr. pulls up to the Guzman's store.

I had that stupid bitch. I fucking had her! Who the fuck was that white boy?

After entering the store and going through the standard search, he enters the back office. He sees Marco raise his head from the Chicago newspaper and look directly at him.

"Junior," Marco says as he stands up to greet him.

"Marco," he replies as they share a handshake, then both sit down.

"How is everything?" Marco asks as he sits back in his chair.

"Well, it could be better, if you must know," he replies.

Marco leans forward and places his elbows on the desk. "How so?" he asks.

"Well, I'm at the mall, messing around, wasting time. I had to meet a guy, and who do I see?" Marco just shrugs his shoulders. "That stupid bitch, Tanya Zaragosa. And she was alone."

Marco's eyes fly wide open. "Did you get her ass?" he asks.

"Not exactly. I had her ass, gun to her back, and I was escorting her outside the mall. Then, out of nowhere, a preppy, pretty boy tackles me to the ground."

"Fuck!" Marco yells, then begins to slam his fists on the table. "Who was this white guy?" Marco yells.

Smoke Jr. just stares and shrugs his shoulders. "I've never seen him before."

"Dammit!" Marco yells again. "What else happened?"

"Me and the white boy were fighting, and then I felt the coldness from the barrel of a gun touch the back of my head."

Marco just shakes his head. "Dammit, we had her ass. She's starting to get too relaxed. We also need to know who this white guy is.

"I know. They got my fucking burner, too. I will see if I can figure out who he is," he says.

"You do that, Junior. Maybe even get a team together and keep a watch on the restaurant to see if you catch that guy there. I know he's doing business with them, or she wouldn't have let him close to her."

"You want me to kill him?" he asks.

"No, we need him alive. With Papi dead, we don't have an insider anymore."

"What makes you think this dude will help us?"

"Everyone has their price, Junior. Everyone does."

"If you say so," he says in agreement.

"Don't worry about my shit. You just find this guy and bring his ass to me alive. You understand me?"

"Yes, Sir. I understand."

"Good, next time I see you, you better have our new friend."

"Yes, Sir" he replies as he gets up and exits the meeting.

Fucking guy wants him alive. I'd like to put a bullet in his forehead for fucking up my plan for that little bitch, Tanya. Yeah, that's what I would love to do.

After leaving the store, he heads toward one of his partner's places. After a short time of stop-and-go traffic in downtown, he finally gets to his partners house, parks his car, walks to the front door and knocks.

"Hold on!" a voice yells from inside the house, and the sound of someone walking towards the door gets louder. The voice inside yells, "Who is it?"

"It's Smoke, Nigga. Open up."

"Hold on," the voice replies as the sound of locks clicking starts. "Come in," the voice says. Smoke enters into the small, ranch-style home. He is greeted by a large six-foot-four, 275 pound overly muscular black man.

"Irving, my main homie. What's up, Family?"

"Take a load off. How can I help you?"

"Well, I got a job for you."

"I'm listening," Irving replies.

"I need help scoping out a restaurant."

"Let me guess, the Zaragosa's?"

"Family, the streets never stop talking. The beef between the Guzmans and the Zaragosas is prime news right now."

Irving nods. "I even heard that the Zaragosa family smoked Lazy.

Damn, Irving is right. This war has been bringing attention to us.

"Why do you need to scope out that spot, anyways?" Irving asks.

"Why? I'm trying to find someone. Some white guy Marco thinks is messing with the Zaragosa's. A really tough dude."

"Do you know his name?"

"No, but I won't forget that face, though. I was beating on his ass a few days ago at the mall when that bitch Tanya stopped it. Plus, if I don't find dude for Marco, I will have my head on a silver platter."

"Well, when do you want to do this?" Irving asks.

"The sooner the better." he replies.

Irving reaches into a stash spot under his couch and pulls out his gun. "Can't be caught slipping," Irving says.

'That's for sure," he replies.

"Let's go."

"Alright, but Irving--Marco wants the dude alive."

"I got you, Family. I won't use it unless I need to."

They get into Smoke's rental car and head to the restaurant. They park close, but far enough away to avoid being spotted. Now, it's a waiting game. A few hours pass and still no sign of the guy.

"Fuck this, we will catch him later," he says.

"Wait...is that him?" Irving says.

"Where?" he asks.

"Right there. He just came from the parking garage. That white dude in jeans and a black T-shirt."

"It kind of looks like him, but I'm not 100% sure. I guess we'll keep an eye out to see when he leaves."

Several hours pass. "Hey, Family, there he is."

"Yeah, that's him, alright. I got a better view of that face. It's got to be him, Family. I haven't seen a white dude other than him go in or come out of that place since we've been here."

"Yeah, I'm almost 100% sure that's our guy. It looks as if he's heading back to the garage, Irving. Go follow him. I'll meet you with the car on the side of the garage. We'll tail him and see where he goes."

"He's going alright, Smoke. I'll meet you on the side of the garage," Irving replies, then gets out and makes his way to the garage. While waiting, Smoke Jr. moves the car over to the side alley next to the parking garage. Minutes feel like hours as he waits for Irving to come back. Several minutes later, Irving comes to the meet spot.

"I got him, Family. He's in a blue and black smart car. He's coming out; pull up there by the street. He should come out very soon," Irving replies.

Smoke Jr. starts up the car and starts to pull forward. He reaches the street, and the blue and black smart car drives past.

"That's him," Irving says.

"All right, all right," he responds. "That thing is small as fuck."

"Yeah, Family, You can fit two of them into a parking spot. I read it in an auto magazine," Irving replies.

They pull out into traffic, but try to stay a safe, two-car distance behind their target. They continue to follow him through the city. As they do, the cars in front of them turn off, leaving them directly behind him.

They pull behind him at a stoplight.

"You hear that?" Irving asks. He turns down the music. "Hear what I hear?"

"A crotch-rocket rumbling, but there isn't any around." Smoke starts to listen closely. "You're right, what the hell is that?"

The light turns green, and the Smart car in front of them peels off, leaving them engulfed in smoke from the tires.

"Fuck, Smoke!" Irving exclaims.

They take off and see him getting on the freeway.

"Damn, Irving. How fast are those things?"

"Not that fast... That shit sounds like a GSX R 1000 motorcycle."

He floors the car on the ramp in hopes of catching up, after chasing the car for a few miles. They catch him getting off the freeway, and follow him to a warehouse district.

"Where the fuck is this dude going?" he says. They finally see him stop in front of a warehouse building.

"I wonder what that is..." Irving asks as they watch a large black man come from inside the building.

"It can't be," he says.

"Who, Smoke?" Irving asks.

"That nigga, Smurf. We got them now, Family," he says as he rubs his palms together.

"I have to tell Marco, okay. Drop me off real quick. I got some business to attend to," Irving says.

"Alright." he replies. They take off and head back to Irving's.

"Here, Family, have some loot for helping me out."

"It's cool, Fam," Irving replies and gestures that he doesn't want it.

"No, you helped me, Irving."

"Alright, I'll take it," Irving replies, then puts the money in his pocket. They say their goodbyes, and he takes off back to the store. After a short time of driving and listening to music, he gets back to the store. Inside, he gets pat searched and let into the office. When he enters, he finds Marco and a Mexican female talking.

"Excuse me, Marco, we need to talk. It's important.

Marco says something in Spanish to the female; she nods, gets up and heads for the door.

"Sit," Marco says. Smoke sits down. "Good news?" Marco asks.

"Yes, we tailed a car to a warehouse to find that guy meeting Smurf, Tanya's boy toy."

"Are you sure it was him?"

"Yes, this white boy is tied in with them directly," he says.

Marco sits back in his chair. "So, are you going to be able to deliver him to me alive?"

"Why do you need to get this guy alive so badly?" he asks. "Let's just kill him."

"Thinking like that is what will be the death of this family."

"What?" he asks. "What you mean?"

"I'm sick of watching our family be ripped apart, one by one. So, you think killing a few of theirs will change something?" Marco asks.

"What about Roberto? They killed him," he responds.

"And they will pay in due time, Junior."

He just shakes his head. "This is why I'm the boss, and you're a gangster. You look out for what's now; I look out for the future of this family. You want to kill now, and ask questions later. That's going to do nothing but stir up more shit."

"That's crap! Your best friend was killed by these fuckers, and you're talking like I'm crazy because I want them dead!"

"If killing a few people is going to make you happy, then do it. But know this, it may attract unwanted attention on the family. You will be dealt with." Junior stays silent. Marco continues. "Junior, don't think I'm not upset about Roberto or Juan and the other family members who have been killed because of this war, but you can't just attack, attack, attack... It's like chess--we have to set up our pieces and attack strategically. If we just attack randomly, they will always have a way out. If we can block them in, they will have nowhere to run. Do you understand what I mean, Son?"

He lets this sink in before responding. "I feel you, but I like to shoot first and then ask questions."

"You do what you're good at--that's enforcing. Just remember, any unwanted attention..."

"I know," he finishes. "I will be dealt with."

Marco lifts his hand and points his index finger upward. "I'm serious... One stupid mistake could crumble this family, Junior. These fucking Zaragosas will get it in the end. We have to sacrifice to gain. It will all work out." Junior nods but says nothing. "Now, work on bringing me this kid. I feel there is more to him than we know."

He nods again. "Yes, Sir."

"Okay, Junior, now get out of here."

He stands up and shakes Marco's hand, then walks out the door.

Marco doesn't want any unwanted attention? Fuck that! The question is who do I smoke first?

He said I'm the enforcer. I'm going to start doing that. Shit around here is going to change.

MINDY

After a few days of relaxing and eating romantic dinners, George and Mindy lie together on a sandy beach and watch the ocean waves roll under a star-filled, cloudless night sky. As she rests her head against his chest, they take in the fresh air and amazing view. He brushes his fingers through the top of her soft hair. She closes her eyes and enjoys the last few moments they have together before she finishes what her cousin asked of her.

So many thoughts run through her head as the sensations through her hair send shivers down her spine and through her body.

"Hey, Mindy," he whispers into her ear. He starts to massage her shoulders.

"Yes?" she replies.

"Have you ever thought about the future?"

"Not really. Why?" she asks.

"Well, I've thought a lot about my future...our future together."

"Has it been good?" she asks.

"As long as you're in it, there is no way it could be bad." She stays silent as he continues to talk. "I just want to spend my time with you. Enjoy moments like these...so peaceful, so breathtaking. I don't care about all the money and materialistic stuff. No money could buy a beautiful woman like you or a moment like this."

"Ah, thank you," she replies with a little giggle.

"What I'm trying to get at, Mindy, is that I have never felt like this about any other woman I've ever met... The feelings I have for you, the love I feel inside of me, the only thoughts that run through my head...are making you my wife and watching a family that we've created grow up."

The sincerity of his words slices into her heart as she listens. A tear starts to collect under her eye, but she wipes it away before it starts to drip down her cheek.

"What do you think, Mindy? How does that sound to you?" he asks.

Mindy says nothing. She un-wraps his arms from around her, turns around and kisses him passionately on the lips.

I can't take this anymore...

She pushes him down onto the sand and straddles him. She begins kissing his neck. She tries to not think about what she must do soon and just tries to enjoy the moment. She works him out of his shirt, and he helps her out of hers.

He slowly slides her bra straps down her arms and unclips her bra, revealing her excited nipples. He starts to lightly nibble and suck on one nipple and then the other. The sensations from him and the slight breeze make her toes curl.

She pushes him back down. She slides down to his jeans, unbuttons them and pulls them off with his boxers tossing them to the side. She then slowly rubs one hand on each leg from his feet up to his belly button. She can tell he wants it by his facial expressions.

She takes him into her hand and slowly licks from the head, down the shaft, to his balls, then back up. She starts to swallow him, and her nose touches his stomach. He lets off a deep moan. He tilts his head back. She continues to suck and lick until he is fully erect.

"I want you deep inside of me," she moans.

He grabs her and rolls her to the side and gets on top. He removes her jeans and panties, then spreads her legs wide. He slowly slides up between her legs, spits onto his hand and wipes it on the head before sliding it deep into her pussy.

He starts to thrust deep into her. She arches her back as she takes every inch of him inside her.

Sensations from his balls hitting her pussy lips fill her body.

"Oh yes, George. Right there," she moans, as she starts to rub on her swollen clitoris. As he thrusts into her, he lets off a deep moan. "No, not yet. Don't come yet, George," she moans. He pulls out and stops.

"I can't help myself. You excite me too much," he says.

"Let me on top," she whispers. He rolls to his back, and she mounts him and starts riding. She leans forward to let him suck on her tits. As she bounces up and down on him, the sensation from his average-length, but thick, dick makes her grab his shoulders. Her body goes into convulsions from her orgasm.

"Oh, God, George. I love you," she moans as she kisses him on the lips.

He lets off one last deep moan and unloads himself deep into her.

"Love you, too," he says, as he pulls her down on top of him.

The next morning, they wake up in the hotel room. George sleeps with his arm around her. All she can do is think about what he said and what happened last night.

Do I have to kill him? I love him. This was stupid of me to come here. I should have listened to Tanya...

"What are you thinking about?" he whispers.

"Nothing, just taking in the moment," she replies.

"So, where are we going today?" he asks.

"A spot I used to go to get away. Great view of the water. One of the best in Columbia."

He smiles and stretches and they get up. They get dressed and eat breakfast. Mindy finishes and puts her plate back on the tray. "I will be right back. I need to use the restroom."

"Okay," he replies.

She grabs her purse from the counter and heads down the hall. In the bathroom, she locks the door and sits on the toilet. She opens her purse and pulls out a small pistol. She stays silent as tears roll down her face and drop on the gun. "I'm sorry," she keeps repeating.

Knock, knock.

"You okay?" he asks.

"Ya, I'm fine. Just a minute," she replies. She wipes the tears from her face and puts the gun back in her purse and flushes the toilet. She meets him back in the main room of their suite. "Are you ready?"

"Yes, let's go," he replies.

They drive twenty minutes in silence before George speaks up. "So, where is this place?" he asks.

"Just up there," she says as she points up to the right.

They pull in, park and begin to walk. She leads, and he follows close behind her. They come up to what looks like a cliff edge, overlooking the water. "Here it is," she says.

"Well, this is nice," he replies and gets closer to the edge of the cliff.

She slowly backs away, pulling her gun from her purse and aiming it at his back. Before she has a chance to shoot, he turns around.

Shock spreads across his face. "What are you doing?"

Her anxiety flares. "Please, just shut up!"

"No," he says as he tries to move.

"Don't move, or I will shoot you...okay?"

He puts his hands up in defense. "Why, Mindy?" he pleads. "I thought you loved me??"

"I do!" she cries.

"But...but...what?" he responds.

"I have to do this."

"Do what? Kill me?" he asks.

"Yes, I can't risk my family's well-being because of you. I'm sorry, George. You know too much."

"That's what this is? The whole thing was a fucking setup?" he yells. "You never loved me, did you?"

She begins to cry harder. "I always have," she yells as she clicks back the hammer on the pistol.

"You better shoot me in the heart, since you already ripped it out of my chest," he yells.

She continues to cry.

"I felt like we were Romeo and Juliet in the end. I guess we really are. There's no happy ending," he says as he pulls off his shirt. "At least tell my parents I said I love them."

She nods. "I love you, Mindy," he says.

She closes her eyes and says, "I love you, too." She puts one bullet, clean, into his upper chest, killing him instantly. He falls back toward the edge of the cliff. She tries to grab him, but it's too late. She falls to the ground and watches his body fall into the water below. She rolls over and sits on the edge of the cliff. She tosses the gun into the water after him.

"I'm so sorry," is all she can say as she places her left hand onto her stomach.

After a short time of sitting and contemplating her next move, she pulls out her phone and calls Tanya.

"Hello, Tanya."

"Hi, Honey," Tanya replies.

"It's done."

"It is? Good."

"Where are you at?" Mindy asks.

"We're in Los Cabos. JJ just bought a house down here."

"What do you want me to do now?"

"Head back to the city. I need you to watch the restaurant for me for a few days until I get back, okay?"

"I will."

"You okay, Cousin?" Tanya asks.

"I'm fine. I'll talk you later," she says, then hangs up.

She finishes the cleanup in Columbia before boarding a plane back to Chicago. After sleeping for several hours, she arrives back in the city. At the airport, she rents a car and heads to the restaurant.

In the office, she finds Quick sitting at Tanya's desk. "What are you doing?" she asks.

He looks up. "Nothing. Why are you back early?" he responds.

"Tanya asked me to run the restaurant while she is gone."

"Okay, good…" Quick says. He gets up.

"Okay, see you later," she replies as she ushers him out of the office.

The rest of the day goes by as normal as ever. She does her daily tasks, but can't get George out of her thoughts. She doesn't know if she ever will.

She leaves and heads to Tanya's to stay. The thought of going back to the apartment she and George had together rips her apart.

After a restless night of fighting her inner demons, she heads to the restaurant early. She calls Quick.

Quick answers his phone saying, "Yes, sister. I'm heading down to the restaurant."

"Are you hungry?" she asks.

"Yes, actually, I am."

"Okay, come down at lunchtime."

"Okay, Sis."

"Okay, Quick. See you soon. I love you."

"Love you too, Sis," he replies, then hangs up.

At the restaurant, she watches as the workers prepare for lunch. She heads back to the office for a second, and returns to find some people coming through the front door.

"We're not open, yet. Come back in about two hours."

The front man says, "Smoke sent us," in Spanish. This freezes her in her tracks.

The second man pulls out a small Mac 10 machine gun and says, "This is a present from our boss, Smoke Jr. and the Guzmans."

Her eyes open wide in horror. This isn't going to end well.

Romeo...my love, I'm coming, I'm coming.

TANYA

Ah, it's Quick...

It's been a few days since her conversation with Mindy. She's boarding a chartered jet with Smurf, JJ and a couple bodyguards when her phone vibrates.

"Yes, Quick," she answers. There isn't a response, only the sound of someone crying. "Quick?" she says again. Still nothing. "Dammit, Quick! Talk! Quit being stupid," she yells into the phone.

"It's Mindy, T," he finally replies.

"What's Mindy? What are you talking about, Quick?" she asks, taking her seat.

"They shot her, T...at the restaurant."

"What? Who did?!" she yells.

"Them fucking Mexicans!"

"Is she alive?" she asks.

"Yes, she's in a coma. They tried to kill her, T," Quick keeps saying as he begins to cry on the phone.

"Relax, Quick. We're on our way back. We will talk when I get there. There is nothing I can do now. Just stay with your sister until I get there, okay?"

"T…"

"Don't worry, Quick, she's going to be okay."

"I know she will. See you soon," Quick replies and hangs up.

She sits back in her chair. Memories of her father and brother fill her mind.

They tried to kill my little cousin…

"Hey, Ma, are you okay? You look like you saw a ghost," Smurf comments.

"I'm fine, just tired," she replies. She may look fine, but her inner demons are ripping at her. The thought of Mindy in a coma puts her in emotional agony.

It's hard for her to sleep during the flight, but after a few hours she manages to force herself to sleep. Even in the safety of a dream, her fears create a realistic scene. Her body shivers as she begins to cry. She remembers her brother's death, seeing his bloody, soulless body lying outside the store… "Hey T, wake up," Smurf says as he nudges her.

"What?" she moans in confusion.

"You are dreaming. Are you okay? You are crying."

"I had a nightmare," she replies.

Smurf just looks at her. "What's really going on? Ever since that call, you've been looking lost...acting lost...and now you're crying in your sleep. So, what's up?"

"Quick's call was to inform me that the Guzmans had shot up the restaurant."

"What?" Smurf replies in a loud voice.

"That's not all. He also said Mindy was there."

"Is she okay?"

"She is in a coma at the hospital," she says with a sad look on her face.

"Don't worry, T. She's going to be okay," Smurf replies as he comforts her.

"I hope so."

"She will be, and I'll pay them fucking Guzmans back for what they did, plus some," Smurf replies.

She sets her head on his shoulder and closes her eyes.

Daddy...why Mindy? Please watch over her. Please...

It feels like only minutes pass before she feels the plane connect back with the earth. Once on the ground, she calls Quick.

"Quick?"

"Hey, Cousin, are you back?"

"Yes, where are you at?"

"We are at St. Jude hospital, room B-11141.

"Okay, I'm on my way," she replies, then hangs up. "Okay, we're

going to St. Jude Hospital." She points at the two largest guards with

them. "You two head to the Miss Kitty strip club and prepare it for a

meeting. We have to use that business to meet, because of recent

events." The men nod and leave.

Another guard accompanies her and gets their parked car in long-

term parking and returns to pick them up. After getting the car all

loaded up, they head down to the hospital.

They make their way through the hospital and find the room. She

pushes the door open to find Quick sitting in a chair, holding Mindy's

hand. The sight of Mindy all wired up to machines makes her crave

revenge.

She walks over and kisses Mindy on the head. "They will all pay for

this...I promise," she whispers. She walks over and hugs Quick. "How are

you holding up?"

"I'm okay," he responds.

"You need a break?"

"No, I'm fine."

"No, you take a break," she says. "I actually need you to contact the guys and set up a meeting at the Miss Kitty strip club."

"When?"

"Tomorrow. I'm going to stay with Mindy tonight."

"Okay, I will set it up."

"Hey, JJ, go with Quick. Smurf, come sit on the couch. It's going to be a while."

Everyone nods, then leaves for their respective locations. She sits in the chair next to Mindy and holds her motionless hand.

This is my fault... I told her to be there...

She leans down and kisses Mindy's hand, softly. "I'm sorry, Mindy... I'm so sorry."

Tanya doesn't leave Mindy's side that night. At around 2:00AM in the morning, the doctor enters to check on Mindy.

"Oh, sorry to bother you, Miss."

"It's okay, Doc," she says. "You think she's going to be okay?"

"It's hard to tell. We removed all the bullets that struck her. This girl was mighty lucky--not one bullet hit a major artery."

"Was she still conscious when they brought her to the hospital?"

"Let me check her paperwork. I wasn't the doctor on duty that day."

"Okay, thank you, Doc. Much appreciated," she says.

He just nods and starts checking all the machines, jotting down notes. The task doesn't take long for him to complete. "I'm finished. She's doing fine, and I will check on that paperwork for you."

"Alright, thanks, Doc," she replies. He turns and exits the room.

She turns and looks at Smurf asleep on the couch. All the recent events make her wonder what her future, their future, the family's future, has in store for them. She takes a deep breath and turns her attention back to Mindy. All the anger and fear for her little cousin slowly starts to consume her and darkens the light in her eyes.

The doctor comes back into the room. "Excuse me, Miss. I have her paperwork."

She stands up and walks over toward the door. "What does it say?" she asks.

"Well, it says the police found her still conscious. While in the ambulance on the way to the hospital, she kept mumbling the word

Junior. Then, she fell unconscious and has been ever since."

She inhales a quick breath. "Thanks, Doc. That is all I wanted to know."

"I hope it helps. Well, I have to get back to work. If you have any more questions, just ask."

"I will," she replies as she shakes his hand. She heads back over to the chair and sits down.

That son of a bitch! Smoke did this! He will pay for this!

The next morning, Quick shows up. "How's she doing?"

"She's doing well. The doctor says all her stuff is good."

"Good, very good," he says. "I set that meeting up for noon at Miss Kitty's."

"Okay, you stay with your sister."

"You don't need me?" Quick asks.

"No, I will let you know how it goes." She turns and sees Smurf staring back at her. "You hungry?" she asks.

"Yeah."

"Let's go to the condo, change and eat before the meeting," she says. She turns back to Quick. "If anything happens, or you need me, you call immediately."

"Okay, T. I will let you know."

She hugs Quick, then kisses Mindy on the forehead and exits the room. Smurf follows Tanya out, where they're greeted by a couple of guards. "Come on. Let's go," she says to them.

After a short time of weaving through traffic, they end up outside the large building . Once inside, Tanya and Smurf shower while the guards cook some breakfast. After they both finish getting ready, they meet the guards in the kitchen for a quick bite before heading to the meeting.

In the car, Smurf's phone beeps. He looks at it for a few moments before speaking. "It's JJ. He says the meeting is ready. They're just waiting on us."

"Good. I will make this quick and to the point," she replies.

They arrive at the strip club and head to the back office. Tanya opens the door and is greeted by all of the major members of the Chicago family.

"Hello, everyone. Thanks for coming on such short notice," she says as she sits down. Smurf takes the spot next her.

An older Spanish man speaks first. "I'm sorry to hear the news of young Mindy."

"Thank you," she replies. She looks around the room, examining all the men. "I called this meeting to inform and update you on the recent events...especially the recent shooting at our restaurant, which left a member of this family in a coma. It has transformed the feud between us and the Guzmans into a full-fledged war."

"Are we sure it was the Guzmans and not just another small crew trying to set off a war between our families?" an older white male asks.

"I checked into it personally, and I found out one of the last things Mindy said before falling unconscious was the word, 'Junior.' Now, we all know Smoke Jr. has come up in the Guzman family recently, and I don't put it past him to pull something like this."

"So, what's our plan of attack?" the white gentleman asks.

"Very simple: Flatten their pockets. We'll do this by hitting all their dope houses. I want all the money and their drugs. I want their houses put out of commission. Do you understand me?" she asks, looking around the room. "I also want Smoke Jr. dead by the end of the month. Anyone who kills him and brings me his body gets an extra $100,000 in cash. Does everyone understand me?" Everyone nods in agreement.

She smiles. "Business continues as normal."

Everyone gets up and exits. Tanya, Smurf and JJ hang back. One of the security guards enters the office as the last man files out. "Excuse me, Miss Zaragosa. Agent Flores is here."

"Send him in," she says.

An older, Spanish-looking man in a suit enters the room. "Miss Zaragosa."

"Hello, Agent Flores. How is my favorite federal agent doing?"

"I'm not doing too badly."

"Why do I have the pleasure of this visit today?" she asks.

"Well, Miss Zaragosa, I came to see you. I've been working with the family a long time. Your father was a dear friend... He helped me get this job." He pauses before continuing. "These recent events, mainly the shooting at the restaurant, have brought both your family and the Guzman family a lot of attention from the bureau."

"So, what are you telling me, Flores?"

"I'm saying...any more attention, and even *I* can't save you. You need to dial back on the violence."

"Thank you, Flores. I'll take that into consideration. Is that all?"

"Yes, that is all," he replies.

"Okay, thank you, Agent Flores. Go enjoy a few private dances on us."

"Thank you, Miss Zaragosa," he replies, then exits the room.

She turns and looks at Smurf. "Smurf?"

"Yes, T?"

"Maybe we should rethink the plan. We don't need any unwanted attention."

"You don't worry about them. You just worry about finding and killing Smoke Jr."

She nods and sits back in the chair. "The plan stays a go, then."

"What about me, Tanya?" JJ asks.

"We need you to keep doing what you do."

"Okay," JJ replies. "Well, I better get going to the lab, then." JJ gets up and goes to leave.

Smurf stands up. "I will walk you out, JJ."

After they leave the room, she takes in a few deep breaths.

I'm not leaving this city 'til I crush them fucking Guzmans!

SMURF

A week has passed since the meeting that was held at Miss Kitty's. So far, so good; the family has continued to conduct business with no interruption from the Guzmans or the feds. The pressure they have put on the Guzmans has helped weaken the family's influence in the Chicago area. The word is out that the Zaragosa family is pissed, and that the only future in sight for the Guzman family is full of bloody bodies.

On this night, Smurf and Quick are getting ready to stick up a known Guzman dope house and put it out of commission, like the others they've hit. His cell rings.

"Who the hell is calling?" he asks as he checks his phone.

"It's JJ."

"Come on Smurf, Man. JJ can wait. Let's hit this place. We know the coast is clear," Quick says.

Smurf puts the phone back in his pocket and nods. "Let's hit this shit and hit it real quick."

They cover up their faces with ski masks and make their way to the back of the house. His phone rings again.

"Fuck, my cell," he says.

"Leave it," Quick says.

Smurf pulls out his phone again. "Fuck, its JJ," he says and answers it. "What, JJ? I'm busy, Dude."

"I'm being followed, I know it," JJ replies from the other end.

Smurf hits Quick on the shoulder and whispers, "Back to the car-- JJ's in trouble."

"Shit! Dammit!" Quick says.

They sneak back to the car. Once inside, he resumes the call. "JJ, are you sure they are following you, Bro?"

"It's just like that last time I met you at the shop. Two black males, about a car length back."

"All right. Where are you at?"

"I was trying to head to the shop to work, when I caught these fools in my mirror," JJ says.

"Okay. Take them on a tour. When we are close, we'll call. Then, take them on four right turns. We'll box them in. Are you still carrying?"

"Yes. I'm packing."

"Okay, because when we get him trapped, fill that car up, you understand?"

"Okay. I'll buy some time. Hurry the fuck up," JJ replies, then hangs up.

He turns to Quick. "You hear that, Quick?"

"We'll box, and then we spray the car. I heard you."

"Do you think it's that nigga, Smoke?"

Quick's anger level shoots up. "I hope so! I'll kill him for what he did to Mindy!"

Smurf nods. "I've wanted to mark that nigga for a minute now," he replies, then pulls over onto the side of the street. He pulls out his phone and calls JJ back.

"Hey, Family. We're on the side street by the shop. Bring them by us, okay? We'll stay on the line."

"Just be ready," JJ replies. A few minutes pass as they stay on the call, but it's silent. No communication.

"Here he comes, Smurf," Quick says. They duck down and let JJ pass. Then, the suspicious car slowly passes, a short time later.

"Take him deep into the industrial district. First stop light, we get them," he says to JJ over the phone.

"Okay," JJ replies.

Smurf watches as JJ pulls to a stop at the first light. The car stops about a car length back from him. Quick flies up behind them and rams into the back of the car. At the same time, JJ hops out of his car and begins firing his gun into the vehicle. Smurf watches as JJ fires shot after shot into the windshield of the car. When the passenger returns fire, JJ runs for cover. The car backs up, running right into Quick. They start firing at the person driving the car as it tries to get away. As the car pulls away, JJ comes out, firing back into the side of the car. The car speeds away, and JJ runs over to Smurf and Quick.

"Are you guys okay?" JJ asks, breathless.

"Yeah. We're good. Are you okay?" he asks.

"Yeah, I'm okay. I saw the passenger's face."

"Did you recognize him?" Quick asks.

"Yep, that was that Smoke dude. It was him for sure."

Quick looks to Smurf. "Fuck, Man! You think he figured out who JJ was?"

He shakes his head. "I don't know. I *do* know they wanted him alive, though, because if they didn't, they would have killed him."

"We need to tell Tanya," Quick says.

"Yeah, she's at the strip club right now," he says. He turns to JJ. "JJ, meet us back at the shop. We need to switch cars. My truck is there.

We'll go see Tanya together."

"Okay," JJ replies and runs back to his car. They speed off to get the trap car back to the shop and park it. Everyone piles into his truck, and they speed away.

"You think they know where the lab is?" JJ asks.

"No, they would have hit it by now," he replies.

They pull up, park and walk into the busy strip club. They walk past the strippers' changing room, and the girls smile and say 'hi' in seductive voices. Finally, at the back door, they go into the office and find Tanya sitting and watching the security camera monitors.

"This better be important," she says.

"T, we had a run-in with Smoke," Quick says.

She sits upright. "Did you kill him?" she asks.

"No."

"Now, that's not what I want to hear," she says.

"T, they were following JJ. It's not safe if they know who he is!" Quick says in defense. "We need to find him a spot to chill for a while. Then we can take care of Smoke."

JJ jumps into the conversation. "Excuse me, Tanya, but I don't need to hide. I'd actually like to help get this Smoke guy. I still owe him for that day at the mall."

"No, JJ. You're needed in the lab, not on the streets," she replies.

"I agree with T," Quick adds.

Tanya looks at them. "Hey, is anyone still staking out the Guzman store?" she asks.

"Yes. Why?" Smurf asks.

"Well, if you had a run in with Smoke, you think he'd be doing the same as you guys: Run to the fort. You'd probably find him there, wouldn't you?" she asks in a forceful tone.

"Maybe," he replies.

"I will call and see," Quick says as he pulls out his phone and walks away.

Smurf, JJ, and Tanya continue to discuss the events. Quick returns.

"I talked to the guys. They said they will call if he shows up, but nothing yet."

"He will be there tomorrow morning; I can almost guarantee he will. Wait until daylight so less attention is drawn to the store. You guys kill him there if he does show. Let's give Marco a present to remember us by," she replies with a smile.

The rest of the night goes by pretty fast. He drops JJ and Quick off at the shop and heads back to the condo to sleep.

The following morning, while he and Tanya are eating breakfast, the silence is interrupted by his phone.

"I bet it's Quick," Tanya says with a smirk on her face then takes a drinks her coffee.

He grabs the phone and looks at the caller ID. "It is Quick."

Damn this girl is good.

Tanya laughs. "See, I told you."

He just shakes his head, smiles, then answers the call. "Hello?"

"Hey, Smurf. I got the call--be ready to go in ten minutes. I'll meet you out front, okay?"

"I'll be there," he replies, then hangs up. He looks at Tanya. "You are right, T. Smoke showed up."

"I knew he would. Don't leave him breathing this time."

"His luck is about to run out," he responds.

"Good. You guys be safe. I love you," she says.

"I love you, too," he replies, then gets up and kisses her softly on the lips.

After getting ready, and all loaded up with ammo and extra clips, he heads down to the street where Quick and JJ are waiting.

"How long you guys been waiting?" he asks, getting into the car.

"About an hour," Quick says.

"Where do they go into this place; is there a back door there?" JJ asks.

"There is, but they use the front to avoid drawing attention. There's a parking lot on the side of the building that they use. I figure we wait for them to leave and try to block the driveway. Then just unload into them," Quick says.

"There's no exit out back…not for a car at least," he says.

"There's a walkway behind the building next to the parking lot that comes out to the street. They parked on the opposite side about half a block down from the store."

"Can you see that far, Family?" he asks.

"No need to. The boys are going to call when he comes out."

They sit and wait, watching people go in and come out, but no call. Finally, after almost an hour-and-a-half of waiting, Quick's phone begins to ring. Everyone focuses their eyes on the store as they see a small group of men, five deep, with a single black man in the middle.

"There he is," JJ says.

Quick starts the car and throws it in gear. The car takes off as he smashes the petal to the ground. They fly up, then come to a screeching stop in the middle of the parking lot entrance.

As Smoke and his men turned to look, JJ aims through the open window and starts letting shots off at them. As the men scramble and duck behind parked cars, the three of them take cover behind their car. Smoke and his goons return fire. The sounds of exploding bullets echo between the buildings.

Quick turns and looks at him. "Watch the store entrance!" he yells.

"What?" he yells back.

"The store! Watch the fucking store!"

"Cover me!" JJ yells.

"What? Where you going?!" Quick yells.

"Trust me, just cover me!" JJ yells again.

Quick and Smurf start the cover fire as JJ takes off running. They watch as JJ runs into the sidewalk, heading to the back of the parking lot.

"Go help him!" Smurf yells at Quick.

Quick nods, and Smurf begins firing random shots, as he starts to follow JJ. Running down the path, Smurf fires a few more shots and empties his clip. He pops out the empty one, loads in a full one then fires off a few more shots. As he stares into the parking lot, he notices out of the corner of his eye two armed men coming out of the store. He turns and shoots at them. One bullet strikes the first man in the chest, and the other hits the second in the shoulder. He continues to fire until he gets a kill shot on the second man. He turns his focus back to the parking lot to see Quick and JJ running back to the car, yelling.

"We got to go!" Quick yells as he runs and gets into the driver seat. JJ climbs into the front passenger seat, and Smurf dives into the back seat. They chirp the tires as they speed away from the scene.

"You guys get him?" he asks.

"Yes, Family! JJ murk'd his ass and put his brains all over the car he was hiding behind," Quick replies.

"Good. We need to tell Tanya. She's still at the strip club. Let's go there," Smurf says.

"First, I'm dropping you off to get your truck, and we need to ditch the car. So, JJ and I will meet you there," Quick says as he pulls over. "Here, Smurf, you only have a few blocks to get to your truck.

"Meet us at the strip club, alright?"

"I'm there," he replies as he gets out and watches them speed away. Smurf starts walking at a fast pace. He reaches his truck, and he puts his stuff into the secret stash spot. As he drives toward the strip club, he starts jamming out DMX's 'Rough Rider Anthem.' He pulls into the partially-empty parking lot, and heads into the club through the back dressing area, then into the back office where he finds Tanya in the same spot as before.

She looks away from the monitors when he comes in. "Hey, Honey, how did it go? Where's Quick and JJ?"

"They are supposed to meet me down here."

"Oh, well, kick back then," she says. He walks over and kisses her, then sits down.

"So, how did it go?" she asks.

"We took care of Smoke's ass. JJ took care of him...really good care. That will make Marco remember us every time he even looks at that grocery store."

Their conversation is interrupted when JJ bursts through the door. They both automatically draw their weapons.

Tanya, scared to death by JJ, starts screaming. "What the fuck, JJ!" she yells.

"Where's Quick?" Smurf asks.

JJ sits down and tries to catch his breath. "Q-uick...Quick...Quick," JJ says, between breaths.

"Relax, Family...calm down. What happened?" he asks.

JJ takes a few minutes to calm down. "Quick got arrested."

"What?" Tanya replies in a loud voice.

"Yes, we went to dump the car. Some cops pulled us over. He told me to take the guns and run for it, and he would draw their attention. So, I took off on foot."

"What did you do with the guns?"

"I dumped them, in pieces, as I ran, tossed the big stuff into industrial-sized dumpsters. They'll never find them," JJ replies.

"Why did they pull you guys over?" she asks.

"I don't know...maybe all the bullet holes in the side of the damn car," JJ replies in a sarcastic tone.

"Hey, don't get smart with me, JJ. I was unaware of that. Actually, tell me what happened at the grocery store, since you're here," she says. "I'd like to hear your side."

A few days later, while Tanya and Smurf work on a plan to get Quick out, Agent Flores bursts through the door of the office. They pull their guns as they watch him walk in.

"Put those things away," Flores says as he comes in and sits in a chair next to the desk.

"How can I help you, Agent Flores?" Tanya asks.

He just shakes his head. "I asked you to do one thing...one simple, fucking thing: Stop the violence...but you do the opposite! You hit the Guzman family in broad daylight, and now you have your little cousin sitting in jail on a multiple murder charge!"

"So, we pay a few dollars, and the case disappears, big deal. That's how it works here," she replies.

"That shit may work with the state, Tanya, but I told you the feds were going to check into this next time. I told you that; now even I can't help you...because he just got picked up by the feds.

"Fuck! How did they hit him with the charges?" she asks.

"They have a material witness that puts him in the car, at the crime scene."

"Can we get rid of her or him?" he asks Flores.

"It's not so simple. They put that person so far deep into witness protection, you'll never be able to find her. And if you do, you will never be able to get her."

"Fuck!" Tanya yells, as she slams her fist onto the table.

"Also, she mentioned that white boy JJ who was there, too. I'd recommend moving him very soon," Flores says.

She rubs her fingers through her hair and keeps repeating, "This can't be happening."

"I have to run, Tanya. If I hear anything else, I will let you know. But, I'd recommend leaving soon, as well."

Tanya takes a deep breath. "Thank you, Agent Flores." Agent Flores nods and exits the office.

"What do we do now?" Smurf asks her.

"We need to figure out how to free Quick, move the family and get Mindy and JJ out of here."

"Where are we going to go?" he asks.

She turns and looks at him. "We're going back to Miami for a while."

MARCO

"Dammit!" he yells as he slams his balled up fists onto the table. He slowly gazes around the office, staring at the family members. "How could an attack like this happen outside of our business...in broad daylight? Anyone? Anyone??" he yells as he stands up and starts to pace the room.

A young Mexican man sitting next to the table speaks out. "Mr. Guzman, sir, it was an ambush.

They took them by total surprise."

"Anyone know a reason on how they were able to get so close to us?" he says in a smartass voice, but everyone stays quiet. "Fine, no one else wants to speak."

Another Mexican man speaks up. "Mr. Guzman, I feel we need to worry more about how to attack back, then stress over the recent event."

"Finally, something I've been waiting to hear. What to do next," he says. "No one comes in and disrespects us like Tanya Zaragosa and her family just did a few days ago. I want her and that nigga boyfriend of hers lying dead on this table by the end of the month. And you better not fail me!"

"If we could kill Alberto and Mario, we can definitely take out that snotty little bitch and the rest of that family," the second man says.

Another man close to him poses another question. "What about business, sir? With both Smoke Sr. and Smoke Jr. gone, it will be hard to reconnect with the black distributors."

"Who needs them?" he yells. "Keep supplying the Mexicans, the whites, and the few Asian families that we have to just stay afloat! Our main focus is to kill off that bitch Tanya and the rest of the Zaragosa family! Anyone have a problem with my orders?" he says in an angry tone. He looks around to see everyone shake their heads. "Okay, good. Get out of here and don't return unless you're bringing Tanya and Smurf's dead bodies to me."

The group vacates the office and he sits back down at his desk. Amid the new silence, his mind drifts.

I miss my boy...Juan...Roberto...and now Smoke Jr. Good men gone at the flick of fingers. How did it come to this? I thought this bitch would have folded under pressure, but she's gotten stronger.

He sits back in his chair, pulls out a cigar from his cigar box on the table, and lights a match. He takes a few puffs and blows out large smoke rings. As he does this, he says "For all or nothing!"

A few weeks pass and there are still no dead bodies to account for. While having a meeting with his new lieutenant in his office, the sound of a car crashing through the doors echoes. He turns to see a line of SWAT-dressed FBI men rush in with assault rifles drawn.

"Get down! Get down!" they yell.

Marco slowly raises his hands off the desk. "I want to see your warrant!" he yells.

A Mexican man comes forward wearing an FBI jacket. "Señor Guzman?"

"Yes, where's your warrant?"

The man smiles, pulls a paper from his vest pocket, and slams it on to the desk. "You're wanted for questioning about the recent shootings that happened outside your grocery store."

He glares at the man. "I want my lawyer!"

"You'll be able to speak with him soon," the man says, then walks away.

Marco is put in handcuffs and escorted out to a waiting GMC Yukon. After being brought to the federal building and led to a holding room, he waits until his lawyer Martinez arrives. He has to wait another half hour before Martinez walks in his room.

"Sorry I took so long, Marco. I sped down here as fast as I could once I got the call from one of your guys. Are you alright?"

He shrugs. "I'm fine. I'm being detained for that recent shooting outside of the store."

"Don't worry, we will get this taken care of," Martinez says as he gets up and leaves the room.

He returns with two agents and they sit down around table.

The Mexican agent says, "I'm Agent Cindelle and this is Agent Robertson. We have a few questions we would like to ask you. Why did the shooting happen?"

"I don't know why," he replies.

"Really? Associates of yours were killed in your business parking lot and you don't know why?" Cindelle asks.

"I couldn't tell you. I was outside at the time."

"We noticed you have video cameras."

"Would like the tapes? They're fake," he responds.

"The cameras are fake? I highly doubt that," Cindelle says.

"Yes, Agent Cindelle. They are fake props; not real," he says in an irritated voice.

"Why would a person put fake cameras at a place of business?"

"It looks better with them. It looks well secured. They made you think they were real, didn't they?"

"I guess so, Mr. Guzman. We are trying to find out any information on why a known cartel member would attack your people."

"I have no idea," he responds.

"Dammit!" Cindelle yells as he slams his fist on the table. "We know who you are, Marco Guzman! Give us what we want!"

Martinez steps in. "I think this questioning is over, Agent Cindelle. Is my client under arrest?"

Cindelle sits back in his chair and glares at them. "No, you're free to go."

Marco and Martinez get up and exit the room without another word and make their way to the car.

"Come on Marco, I'll give you a ride," Martinez offers. They get in the car and begin to drive.

"Now, Marco, a word of advice."

"What's that?" Marco says, obviously irritated.

"Now that you know the feds are breathing down your neck, just remember to cross your T's and dot all your I's."

"Yes, I'm aware of that. Thanks, Martinez."

They arrive at the store. They arrive at the store and he gets out. "Thank you."

"Yes, of course. Anything else happens, you call me," Martinez replies. He closes the door and watches Martinez drive away.

He walks into the store and back towards the office. Marco stares at the door laying on the ground.

It's time for me to go. The city is getting too hot, too quick. I need to regroup and think of a new strategy.

He searches through the office and grabs up anything worth value to him. After twenty minutes of rummaging through the trashed office, he pulls out his phone and calls his driver.

"Hello?" a man answers.

"Yes, come pick me up at the store. Also, get a hold of the people at the airport and let them know to have the jet ready to take off in one hour."

"Yes, sir. I'll be there soon," the man replies. He ends the call.

In the car, he thinks back on the recent events. His anger mounts.

Fucking, bitch...stupid...fucking, bitch.

He gets to the airport and boards his jet. The pilot walks into the passenger cabin and greets him.

"So where to, Mr. Guzman?"

"Mexico City. Take me back to Mexico City."

"Yes, sir," the pilot says.

Within minutes, they take off. He looks out the window to see the skyline of Chicago. As he stares at the city he says stays silent. As the plane levels off, he sits back in his chair.

Tanya Zaragosa, you might have won the battle, but I will win the war.

He closes his eyes, leans back in the reclining seat, and goes to sleep.

TANYA (A month after the shooting)

While sitting at the hospital, watching over Mindy, Tanya is interrupted by the doctor. "Excuse me, I didn't know anyone was in here."

"It's okay, Doc. You doing some checking up?"

"Yes, just checking her vitals," he says, scanning the monitors and writing on his clipboard.

"Hey, Doc, can I ask you a question?"

He finishes writing and looks up. "Yes, of course. What is your question?"

"I'm hoping to move my cousin closer to her family... Is it possible to move her?"

"Where exactly are you trying to move her?"

"Miami, Florida," she replies.

He takes a deep breath. "Honestly, it might be hard to move her that far because of her condition."

Tanya's phone begins to ring. "Excuse me, I have to take this."

"No worries, go ahead."

She looks at the screen and sees that it's Smurf. "Hello, Honey," she says.

"Hey, T. Where are you at?"

"I'm at the hospital with Mindy," she replies.

"Good, because your Uncle Omar and Aunt Lannett just walked into the condo."

"Oh, okay. Bring them down here, please?'

"Okay, we will be down there soon."

"See you soon," she replies and hangs up. She starts rubbing Mindy's arm. "Honey, your parents are coming. They will be here soon," she says gently. A few hours pass.

"Hello," a voice says from the doorway. Tanya turns and sees her Aunt walk in.

"Hello, Auntie," she says.

"Hello, Honey," her aunt says in a sad voice. She looks from Tanya to her daughter lying in the bed. "Oh my God, my baby girl," she says as she runs to her daughter. "Oh, Honey, I'm so sorry," she says as she begins to weep at Mindy's bedside.

Smurf and Omar enter the room.

"T," Smurf says.

"Hi, Honey."

"Hello, Uncle," she replies as she gets up and hugs him.

"Honey, are you okay? How's my little girl doing?"

"The doctor says she's doing very well," she replies. She watches her uncle walk over and kiss Mindy on the forehead.

"Excuse me," Omar says. "Tanya, I need to talk to you alone."

"Alright, let's take a walk."

The two of them leave and walk down the hall to an empty room.

"What is it, Uncle?"

He closes the door behind them. "We have a major problem."

"What is it?" she asks.

"There was a shooting that happened a few weeks ago, involving Quick. I told you in the message."

"Yes, I remember."

"Well, it's been brought to my attention by the feds."

"We need to split for a while and let things cool down. I also talked to the doctor about moving Mindy to Miami, and he said that she couldn't be moved in her condition."

"That's fine. Your auntie will stay here and take care of your cousins. You go do what you need to do," he replies.

"Thank you, Uncle. We're planning to go back to Miami."

"Good. Your mom is all alone down there at the house, so you could stay with her for a while."

"I will."

"Okay, let's get back to Mindy," Omar says.

"All right," she replies. They both hug and walk back to the room.

As they enter, she pulls Smurf to the side. "Call JJ and tell him to meet us at the condo," she whispers.

"Okay," Smurf replies.

Tanya's eyes examine the room. She watches her auntie weep over Mindy. All she can do is think about how it's her fault Mindy was there. It's her fault Mindy was shot.

Smurf returns and whispers in her ear, "He's on his way."

She nods. "Auntie, Uncle," she says. They turn from Mindy to look at her. "We need to leave.

You guys going to be alright?"

"Yes, we are fine, Tanya. If we need you, we will call," Omar says.

She nods then they exchange hugs and goodbyes. Tanya and Smurf leave the hospital and head back to the car.

"So, why are we meeting JJ at the condo?" Smurf asks.

"Because we are leaving, and he needs to do the same."

"What about Quick? We can't just leave him to rot in jail."

"He's coming, too."

Smurf just gives her a blank look and stays quiet. He starts the car, and they leave the hospital parking lot.

Upon arriving at the condo, they are greeted by JJ in the lobby. They all walk to the elevator together and up to the condo. Once inside, they head to the living room and sit.

"So, what's up," JJ asks.

"I needed to talk to you. Shit's getting too hot here. We need to bounce for a while."

"How long is awhile?" JJ asks.

"Could be a year, ten years, maybe even forever."

"What? Forever? What about my parents? My family!" JJ begins to yell.

"JJ, I understand your concern, but by you leaving, you're actually protecting your family. Marco isn't dead and he knows of you. Plus, with your involvement in the shooting outside of the store, he might want to retaliate and attack friends and family.

JJ rubs his head. "Can I at least say goodbye?"

"You're a big boy. Do what you want, but don't tell them where you are going. Just let them know that you're going away for a while."

"What about Quick?" JJ asks. "We can't just leave him."

"Don't worry about him, he's going to be fine. Just make sure you get out of town soon. Call us when you get to Los Cabos."

"Okay, I will be on the next plane flying south."

"Oh, hey, if Smurf calls and says you need to move, do it."

"Where to?" JJ asks.

"We will meet in the Florida Keys, but that's only if he lets you know."

"Alright, I got you. So, I guess this is it, huh?" JJ says.

"Only for now, Family," Smurf replies.

JJ just shakes his head and stands up. "Well, give me a hug since I'm leaving," he says to Tanya.

She smiles and hugs him.

"Tell Sissy and Carlos I say 'hello,'" she says.

"I will."

Smurf holds out his fist. "JJ, it's been real, Family."

"Yes, Smurf. I consider you a true friend." He bumps Smurf's fist with his.

"Don't be getting all emotional on me now," Smurf says in his deep voice.

JJ laughs. "No, for real, though. I consider you all family."

"Good, because you're always going to be a part of this family," she replies.

He just shakes his head and says, "Okay, I'm going to go. I will call you when I reach Los Cabos."

"Good, have a safe trip," she replies.

JJ opens the front door one last time, looks back and waves, then closes the door behind him.

"T," Smurf says.

"Yes, Honey?" Tanya asks.

"Why did you say 'if I call him that he needs to meet us in the keys'?"

"So he can pick up Quick," she replies.

"Yeah, we will see how his case goes."

"If it's not looking good, we're going to need to figure out an escape plan."

He eyes her. "You're crazy, has anyone told you that?" Smurf asks.

She laughs. "My whole life, I've been told that. I must be crazy, huh?"

He begins to laugh. "I guess, but that's why I love you."

She smiles and gives him a kiss on the lips. "I love you, too, Smurf." She then pulls out her phone and calls her mother.

"Hello, Mama."

"Hey, Honey," her mom says.

"Are you doing okay, Mom?"

"Yes, I'm okay. It's kind of lonely in this big house."

"Okay, well, Smurf and I are coming soon to visit. We'll keep you company."

"Okay, that's great! I can't wait," her mom says with excitement.

"Me either, Mom. Me either."

A few days pass and there's still no call from JJ. Finally, after four days, while Tanya and Smurf are sitting on the couch, his phone rings. It's JJ.

"Hello? You make it?" Smurf asks as he puts JJ on speakerphone.

"Yes, I'm good, Bro. I've been busy with Sissy since I got here."

"Good, that girl will keep you busy, for sure," Tanya says, laughing.

JJ begins to laugh as well.

"JJ, just remember what I told you."

"I know, I know. If or when I get the call."

"Yes, just don't forget."

"I won't. Well, Sissy is ready."

"Put her on," Tanya says.

"Okay, hold on."

"Hello," Sissy says into the phone.

"Sissy!" Tanya says an excited voice.

"Hey, girl," Sissy replies.

"Hey, you take care of him, okay?" Tanya asks.

"Come on, girl, you know me. Don't worry! He's in good hands."

"I know he is in very good hands, but I will let you guys go. Take care," she says.

"You too, Tanya. Take care," Sissy replies and hangs up.

"Well, looks like he's going to be all right," Smurf says, putting his phone away.

"Yes, Smurf. He's going to be fine...just fine."

"So, what's next, T?"

"Now, we just wait to see what happens with Quick."

Smurf shakes his head, smiles, and then wraps his arms around her. She lays her head against his chest, and all she can think about is the family and Quick.

How are we going to get him out of this if things go south for Quick?

She stays silent as they watch TV, but the thought keeps playing over and over in her head. Her breath catches when the solution finally comes to her.

I know exactly how to break him out...

JJ

The sky is cloudless as the morning sun beams down. A gentle 80° breeze blows, creating sensations that make skin feel as if it were being kissed gently by the lips of an angel. The clear, blue ocean and white sands are breathtaking.

"JJ, would you mind rubbing some suntan lotion on us?" the beautiful brunette says with a seductive grin.

He removes his sunglasses and looks at the blonde and brunette beauties.

"Sure, Sissy."

Both ladies remove their bikini tops and prepare themselves for the touch of his strong hands.

In most men's opinions, he is living a fantasy beyond his wildest dreams. He is young, wealthy and very powerful. Yet, he is unhappy. He owns a very large oceanfront villa tucked away in Los Cabos. It's an amazing house with architectural design that would make some of the richest people on the planet jealous.

The house is located on 2 acres of oceanfront land. It takes up 10,000 square feet, with five bedrooms and five-and-a-half bathrooms.

Three of those bedrooms are in the main house, and the other two are in the guest house. No detail was overlooked when the house was built. The master bedroom features a large wall of pocket doors that open to a one-hundred-foot, private ocean frontage, but that wasn't enough. He even has a large outdoor living space, which contains a large pool with swim-up bar, outdoor kitchen and a large movie theater. He also has a garage where he keeps his transportation, which includes a mix of exotic cars.

His real love is his home on the water; an eighty-five-foot yacht with six staterooms, an elevator and a wide open deck for large gatherings. On top of the best-of-the-best interior design, it even boasts a helipad with helicopter, in case of emergencies.

In the last two years, he has lived a life that has felt like a rollercoaster ride. After all he's seen and done, never would he have imagined that a paradise such as his getaway spot would serve as his prison. Psychologically, it tortures him to know that what he wants most in the world can never again be obtained. He is in too deep. If he could go back to his old life and be a regular college kid again, he'd give up all these luxuries and all of this money...just to be free.

The irony is that he is not in prison, but rather, has imprisoned himself within his own world. Life has forced him to shut the rest of the world out. It's safer that way, and it's the only way to protect his loved ones. What he wouldn't give to see his mother and father again.

His phone rings, interrupting his thoughts.

"It's time to move," the familiar voice says over the phone.

He has come to trust Smurf and doesn't hesitate to answer. "I will be ready," he says, then disconnects.

He looks again at the beautiful women as they kiss and touch each other. He puts his aviator sunglasses back on and leans back in his chair. The thought that comes to his mind is probably the most repetitive he has endured for a long as he can remember.

How did it come to this?

He inhales the salty air and releases it slowly. "Sorry, Sissy, but we have to go."

"What do you mean?" she asks.

"I got that call I told you about awhile ago."

"Oh, okay," she replies.

He turns around, heads into the house and calls the crew for his yacht. He tells them be on board in one hour.

JJ heads to the bedroom that he and Sissy share and begins packing all that he plans to take. He pulls copy of the picture of his family off his dresser, and puts it in his luggage. After the blonde girl leaves, Sissy comes back into the bedroom.

"When are we coming back?" she asks.

"I don't know, so just pack what you need." Sissy nods and hurries to get packed. He grabs her arm as she turns. "I'm going to the boat," JJ says.

"I will meet you there, okay?" she replies.

He kisses her and leaves the room. He walks through the kitchen and down to the waiting yacht.

As he boards, he is greeted by some of the crew.

"Is everyone here," he asks.

"Not yet, but in twenty minutes we will be ready, Mr. Jepenski," the Captain says.

"Okay, good," JJ says as he hands his luggage to one of the crewmembers. He makes his way to the upper level of the yacht and takes a seat on the outside furniture. Sissy shows up minutes later and sits next to him.

"We're ready," the Captain says.

"Okay, let's get going!" JJ commands.

"Where to, Mr. Jepenski?"

"To the Keys, Captain. The Florida Keys."

"Okay, sir," the Captain replies, then walks away.

Sissy turns to JJ. "Where are we going after the Keys?"

"I don't know," he responds. "Isn't Carlos back home in Amsterdam?"

"Yes, he went back a couple of weeks ago," she replies.

"Hmm, Europe sounds nice to me. I bet Amsterdam is nice around this time," he replies. He pulls out his phone and calls Carlos.

"Hello?" Carlos answers.

"Carlos."

"What are you doing, JJ?"

"Nothing, what's going on? How's the weather in Amsterdam?" he asks.

"It's beautiful, why?"

"Because we're on our way."

"Really? Okay...just to visit or are you taking me up on that offer?"

JJ goes quiet, then says, "Let's just say America got a little taste of what I have to offer. I think it's time for the rest of the world to get a taste."

Carlos laughs. "Okay, I will have a house waiting for you.

"Okay, Carlos, we will see you soon."

"Sounds good, JJ. See you guys soon," Carlos replies and hangs up.

After finishing the call, JJ calls Smurf back on the number he just called from.

"Hello," Smurf says.

"Hey, Bro. I'm in route."

"Okay, good. I will be seeing you soon."

"Yes. Hey, Smurf?"

"Yeah?"

"It's good to hear your voice, again. I've been waiting for your call since I got down here."

"Are you ready to get back into the swing of things?" Smurf asks.

"Fuck yeah! I was going broke, Bro."

"I heard. A helicopter, huh?" Smurf asks as he begins to laugh.

JJ begins to laugh, as well. "You never know when you're gonna need it."

"I hope you can fly that thing, because if I ever need a ride, you better come get me."

"Don't worry, Bro. I got you."

"Alright, Family, I'm gonna get off this thing. I will be seeing you, alright bro?"

"I will see you soon." JJ replies. He sits back on the couch with his arm around Sissy. He pulls her close and says, "First, we stop in the Keys and pick up Quick. Then, it's off to Amsterdam."

She just looks at him and smiles. She lays her head on his chest and slowly rubs back and forth across his hard stomach. He smiles.

Maybe life isn't as bad as I thought, after all.

QUICK

"Quick," Smurf says. "Yo, Quick!"

"Hey, Family."

"Are you alright?" Smurf asks, nudging him.

"Huh? What? What's up?" he replies.

"Dude, Family, you are looking like you are lost in space. Are you alright?" Smurf asks.

"Man, I'm just thinking."

"About what?" Smurf asks.

"Shit, Family, everything... the last year I spent in jail, beating that murder rap...but now they want to hang me for a gun case and give me the max, which is a dime apiece."

"These feds are wild. You think you got them beat, and they slap you with some more shit."

"I was lucky they even let me bond out once they dropped the murder charges," Quick says, still in a slight daze.

"Them niggas are trying to give you ten years in Fed?"

"Yeah, Family, they want me to lay it down, but they're crazy!"

"Ten years for guns they never even found? Sounds like simple shit to me, Cuz."

Quick nods. "Definitely is, Smurf. Definitely is."

"So, what you gonna do?"

"I'm about to say fucking dip out."

Smurf just nods, but doesn't reply.

"Where we going, anyways?" he asks.

"Well, Family, a lot has changed in the last year. After everything went down, we split the family up for a while...let shit cool down for a minute."

"Yeah, my mom told me on a visit that you and T moved down here to Miami."

"Yeah, we've been kicking it for a while...just keeping a low profile."

"What about JJ? Where is he?"

"In Los Cabos. He's been doing the same, just chilling."

"He doing alright?" he asks.

"Oh, yeah. Sissy has been taking care of him.

"That's good." There's a moment of silence before he continues. "You still never told me where we are going."

"I need to make a stop in the Keys real quick," Smurf says.

"For what?"

"It's a surprise," Smurf replies.

He gives Smurf a confused look, but doesn't say anything. They continue to drive out of South Florida and cross the long bridge that leads to the Keys.

He looks out at the water and stares at the wide-open, blue ocean.

Do I really want to go to prison for eight-and-a-half years for simple shit, gun charges?

They finally reach the Keys and drive into town. He watches as people walk down the sidewalks and into stores.

"Everyone looks so happy," he says under his breath. The decision he's being forced to make is one the most stressful and life-changing he's ever had to endure. He weighs the pros and cons of the situation as more people and shops fly by.

The car finally pulls to a stop.

He looks around, more confused than ever. "What are we doing at a marina?" he asks.

"Come on," Smurf says as he gets out of the car and starts to stroll down the walkway at the docks. He follows Smurf into the docks. "There it is!" Smurf calls.

"There it is?" he says, still confused. He watches as Smurf heads toward a large white-and-black yacht with a small helicopter sitting on it. "You guys bought a boat?" he asks. Then, he sees the name of the boat on the back. ⬚he ⬚liss ⬚ne.

He follows Smurf onto the boat and up a flight of stairs to the second deck of the yacht. Then, a familiar, voice says, "Smurf, Quick!"

Quick looks up to see JJ stand up from the table he was sitting at.

"JJ," he says.

He sees Smurf shake his hand and ask, "How was the trip?"

"Good, real good," JJ says, then turns and looks at Quick.

"Hey, Bro. How's my favorite brother from a different mother doing?"

"It's good to see you, Bro," JJ says, then hugs him.

"What's up, Family? Is this yours?"

"Yes, what do you think?"

"This shit is hot, Family! And you have a personal helicopter," Quick says, laughing.

"Yes, I'm still learning how to fly it, but I will get it down. Come on and sit down you guys. Are you thirsty?"

"Yes," they both reply.

"I will take a Henny and Coke," Quick says.

"Make that two," Smurf replies, as they all sit down.

A female crewmember comes over. "Hey, get a Henny and Coke for these two, please," JJ says to the lady. She nods and walks away. "So, Smurf, where is Tanya?" JJ asks.

"She's running behind, but she'll be here in about an hour. Where's Sissy?" Smurf replies.

"She's lying down right now. I will get her up when Tanya gets here. How's Mindy doing?" JJ asks.

"Well, she came out of the coma, but she is paralyzed from the waist down. Did you know she was pregnant?" he asks JJ.

JJ's eyes widen. "I didn't know she was."

"Yes, but she had a miscarriage."

"I'm sorry to hear that, Quick."

The crewmember comes back with a tray. "Excuse me, Sir, here are your drinks."

"Thanks," both Quick and Smurf reply, as they take them from her.

The young woman smiles and says, "You're welcome," then walks away.

"Oh, I almost forgot," Smurf says.

"What's that," JJ replies.

"I took care of your mother and father on all holidays and birthdays. I sent them cards, flowers, and money from you."

"Really? I appreciate that, Smurf. I really do," JJ replies.

"Not to worry, JJ. They are doing well. I have people watching them, to keep them safe while you are away."

"Thank you, that means a lot to me. You guys, they are all the family I have. I really miss them and want to see them."

"In due time, JJ," Smurf replies. "But, life in the Windy City is still hot, hot, hot. We did finally run Marco Guzman and his crew out of the city. But we ran ours out, as well."

"Hello," a female voice says from behind JJ. Everyone turns and looks as Sissy walks in and takes a seat next to JJ.

"You guys remember Sissy, right?" JJ asks.

"Well, I met her at long time ago," Quick says.

"Well, Sissy, if you don't remember--that is Smurf, Tanya's boyfriend, and this is Quick, Tanya's little cousin."

"I remember Smurf," she says.

"How are you?" Smurf asks, taking a gulp.

"I'm good, and it's good to see you."

"Likewise," Smurf replies.

She turns and looks Quick. "It's nice to see you again, also."

"You remember me?" he asks.

"You were just a little boy, but yes I do. Now, where's my girl at?" Sissy asks.

"On her way," Smurf replies.

"Okay, I'm going to go change," she says. She kisses JJ on the lips and goes back inside the yacht.

"You got yourself a keeper there, JJ," Smurf says.

"Yeah, Bro, I think I'm going, marry that girl."

Everyone begins to laugh, when another female voice says, "What's so funny?" Everyone turns towards the back of the boat to see Tanya walk onto the deck.

"T," JJ says as he stands up. Smurf and Quick slowly stand, and they all exchange hugs.

"I've missed you, Quick," she says.

"I've missed you too, Cousin," he replies.

She hugs Smurf and kisses him, and they all sit down at the table.

"How have you been, JJ? I can't believe it's been a year already! Where's Sissy?"

"Life's been good. Sissy is changing--she'll be back soon," JJ replies.

"How are you two doing?" she asks.

"Great. Really great, actually. Thank you, Tanya, for introducing us!"

"No problem, she's a great girl. By the way, I love the yacht. I think the helicopter is definitely you."

JJ laughs. "You know me--I love to be different."

"True story," Smurf replies and starts to laugh, as well.

Sissy returns from changing and walks up to the table. "There's my girl!" she yells as she runs over to Tanya. They give each other a big hug and sit down.

Tanya asks, "So, JJ, what are your plans?"

"Well, I'm actually planning to head to Amsterdam and set up shop there. It's time for the world to experience my work."

"That's good! Real good! I think we're ready to give it to the world," Tanya replies.

"Yes, Carlos is going to help set me up to mass produce it for both pill and powder form, but I still need an assistant."

Tanya turns and looks at Quick. "So, what is your plan? Stay or go?"

He looks around the table. "Fuck the feds. I'm like the gingerbread man--got to catch me if they can."

"You know, if you go, you most likely won't be coming back," Tanya replies.

"It's either eight-and-a-half years in prison or out enjoying my life. Well, I'll make them come find me, then.

"Then, it's settled. Amsterdam it is," Tanya says.

"Good, I was hoping you would like my idea! The world will soon be our playground. It won't even know what hit it," JJ replies.

The group continues to drink and enjoy the rest of the day on the yacht. And at the end of the night, after all the drinking is done and over, after everyone gives each other hugs and says their goodbyes, JJ and Quick stand looking out onto the open ocean from the upper deck.

"Are you ready? There's no turning back," JJ says.

He looks at JJ. "Ready as I will ever be, JJ."

"Just wait, Quick. If you like Chicago, you're going love Amsterdam! Trust me, I already know." JJ smiles and pulls out his cell phone to make a call. Quick overhears JJ talking on the phone and hears him say,

"Alright, Bro, it's a go. We are on our way." JJ finishes the call and puts the phone back in his pocket.

Quick looks at him. "So are we good, JJ?"

"Yes, Sir!"

Quick takes a deep breath as he continues to stare out at the ocean. "Amsterdam, here we come!"

ABOUT THE AUTHOR

B. A. Talarico was born in Des Moines, IA. After having success with his original novel Bliss, he continued to write creating his second novel in the Bliss Trilogy. B. A. knew after his first novel hit shelves this was his calling and needed to continue on his path with his writing career.

*Smurf also requested not to be mentioned in the Bio.

You can find more information about B.A. Talarico and the Bliss series at this sources:

Website: www.blissthebook.com

Instagram: @blissthebook

Facebook: https://www.facebook.com/thebookbliss

Twitter: @blissthebook

Also please if you enjoyed my novel Bliss 2, please take a few minutes to go and write your review. Thank You!

www.ingramcontent.com/pod-product-compliance
Lightning Source LLC
Chambersburg PA
CBHW070207260626
47160CB00002B/482